Boomerang

Also by Eli Makover

The Longest Visit: A Memoir

Boomerang

A NOVEL

ELI MAKOVER

Full Court Press
Englewood Cliffs, New Jersey

First Edition

Copyright © 2025 by Eli Makover

All rights reserved. No part of this book may be reproduced or transmitted in any form or by any means electronic or mechanical, including by photocopying, by recording, or by any information storage and retrieval system, without the express permission of the author, except where permitted by law.

Published in the United States of America
by Full Court Press, 601 Palisade Avenue,
Englewood Cliffs, NJ 07632
fullcourtpress.com

ISBN 978-1-953728-46-3
Library of Congress Control No. 2025912049

Editing and book design by Barry Sheinkopf

Cover art, "California Palm, Calabasas, CA, 2019," courtesy Barry Sheinkopf

To my grandchildren, with all my love

Binyamin, Neema, Shlomo, Racheli,
Chen, Noam, Yakov, and Ziva

CHAPTER ONE

NORA

LATE NOVEMBER: I COULD HEAR the elevator, no longer hushed in the background, louder than ever—as if it was the first time I'd ever noticed that bizarre sound of metal and hydraulics merging with the restlessness of my own breath. A young girl emerged from the elevator doors. Her eyes were green behind small pink glasses that framed her face. There was a sadness about her, though. Before I introduced myself, I noticed her bright yellow sweater, and for some reason it seemed like a whole new color. Through the years, I'd always felt a deeper connection to children. Emilie never understood that about me. I had always felt she was in fact a bit jealous when it came to my natural bond with the young. And despite my discernibly masculine disposition, children seemed to take a liking to me as well, as if we were on the same level. They could sense that I was not just a man inside my humble exterior.

Not having had a child with Emilie myself, I guess you could say that something had always been missing from my life. When I met Nora, she and I had a special affinity that I hadn't anticipated. Maybe I reminded her of her own father?

"Well, hello there, child. My name is Joseph. And what is it that they call you?" The little girl was reluctant to answer and instead responded by telling me I was a stranger, even if I was her new neighbor. She eventually warmed up, though, and announced her name. Her eyes lit up, and I in turn responded,

"Eleanor! May I call you 'Eli,' by chance? Welcome to the building. It's a bit chilly this morning, don't you think?"

"My mom calls me Nora because it has two syllables instead of three. And my friends, they call me Eli. Grammy calls me Eleanor, out of respect for the first lady, Mrs. Roosevelt. But. . .I guess you can be my friend too, sir. If my mom says it's okay. And yes, it is cold out today, isn't it?"

I was amused by her demeanor, how intelligent and well spoken she was, as if she had no clear idea that she was just a little girl—one I imagined was seven or eight years old.

Nora, wild-eyed, the girl with the pink glasses, awaited her mother's arrival, dancing clumsily around the men who were slowly transporting the fragments of her life from the moving truck. Past my door. Two bedrooms, $4,000.00 a month. No wonder that the unit had sat there abandoned for almost three months.

I am retired now and divorced for quite a while, so I no longer have to worry about affording a place. But for those who are not in my position, I do feel that great misfortune in the air. It's a smell that cannot be avoided, the idea of not being able to afford enough food because rent is too high. This is the new world, one built without the permission of its inhabitants and middle-class workers. Is Los Angeles worth all of this financial disparity?

I live alone. Mornings I spend playing the piano, fretting at times about my receding hairline and the white hairs that are growing in on my sideburns and, even more these days, across the top my head. I can't pretend I haven't noticed a slight arthritic tremor, which I have feared slowly catching up with me. But it comes.

By noon I've read the paper. I let each week's article lie atop the next; eventually, I'll discard the older ones. I do like when they pile up as they do, though, while the months pass me by.

Then there's Brenner's Hill. I was born here two years after the founding of the State of Israel, directly after it was said that Kasztner had sold his soul to the devil. As a teenager, I excelled in both math and science. And I can't claim I don't have a love affair with chess: in fact, I was indeed a chess champion.

I am hypnotized by these bouts of nostalgia. I let them rush in. Why deny myself the simple pleasure? They say that remembering who you are and where you came from is just as important to your development as growing into each decade. My mother's eyes—she a romantic and the daughter of a local cantor in a small village in Eastern Poland—were a radiant blue, just like mine.

Drifting through my thoughts now, I watch the clouds move beyond the traffic below my balcony. I'll be sixty-one soon, and once in a while I mutter to myself, "Joseph, you're only getting younger as the years go by!" Who am I kidding? But I do rather enjoy staying active, and find myself still in terrific physical shape. My doctor confides to me that, metabolically, I could pass as someone in his forties. This is something one likes to hear from their doctor, especially when I think about turning sixty-five (then comes eighty in the blink of an eye, or so, I've been told. And what would that final decade entail?

My name is Izak Birnberg, but people call me Joseph Brenner. I've been in love once or twice, I'm sure, but in the Seventies love itself was something free and unapologetic. I'd meet a lovely woman, and we'd share very few words, if any. And there were many women, no one looking to get hitched and start a family—a girl would follow me to my piano, and shortly after a few drunken Elton John covers in a bar, we were hot and heavy in the parking lot.

When such encounters ended, I finally settled in quite nicely at a large university in Southern California, where I was supposed to begin furthering my studies. I met Emilie then. She was a fine woman. Sometimes I close my eyes and think back on the moment we first locked lips outside her dormitory, when her skin was less worn by age and uncertainty. She said to me once that she watched her entire world change, in my eyes. That really grabbed me. Plus, she had a great pair of legs and was actually interested in furthering her education. After our bachelor's studies she wanted to work toward her doctorate. How could I turn her down? She was quite a catch.

Often I wish I had looked at her more, played more songs for her on my piano. But I was eager to marry, for no other reason than it appeared to be the right thing to do, as a man— to provide for someone who would give me children one day, as the Eighties were no longer about free love. I needed to secure a future in honor of what my parents had worked so hard at achieving for my own development.

Did Emilie marry me for the same reason? Was it next on her list, what was expected of a young woman in her mid-twenties? After all, I was just an ex-Israeli fighter pilot and a lonesome piano player. She was the one with a real future, or so I thought at that time.

Emilie's family seemed to take some interest in me but, I will admit, not much. They had their own pampered and organized lives, a vast empire of commercial real estate investments. Their world was dinner parties, unrepeatable conversations, expensive attire that I at times found somewhat inappropriate. If you don't perform a certain role, no one will take you seriously, and then what happens? You find yourself rotting behind the veil of a dream that you never imagined you'd fulfill anyway.

I didn't care much for Emilie's family either, although at times I wish that I had felt *some* sort of connection to what appeared to be a family, since my parents were still so far away.

At times I even felt, reluctantly, that Emilie could have found someone better for whom she was at her core. Should I have instead run away with another musician, one who could see me truly?

Whatever it was we had, it was only after six years invested in our marriage that Emilie decided she had found much more solace in the bottle than in our partnership. And I can't argue that I ever disagreed with her decision to choose otherwise. But I've said too much already, for if I paint myself too loathing of the past, you may not be as interested in my story.

No time for regrets. I have some new friends to tend to. Maybe no real time has passed at all, just a minute or two, while everything from all of those years plays its solemn dirge to my subconscious, distracting me once again.

"Mom? Mom! Look, our new neighbor!" the child at my feet called out that day, excited to share me. I wanted to be sure I was paying attention. *Be stoic, Joseph. Your emotions do not govern you.*

"So, this is my mom. She's an indeepenant, an indahpendant. . .woman! She doesn't like when I tickle behind her knees. . .like this!" Eleanor ruffled her mother's hair then proceeded down to her knees, but the woman was quick on her reflexes and scooped the girl off her feet and into her arms. The two looked into one another's eyes for a moment, smiling deeply, and Nora stuck out her tongue, then hid her face in mother's nest of soft, snow-like hair. "Mom, I wanted to tell you that this is the man that lives here too. . .what's your name again, sir?" she mumbled, her eyes closed behind the pink glasses as she faced where I stood. I laughed for a second, then leaned in to introduce myself.

"No need at all for 'sir,' please. My friends call me Joseph," I said as I extended my hand to meet the mother's as she was setting the girl down.

Instead of shaking my hand, though, she nervously ran both of hers through her hair as she begged me to forgive her for how she looked after the long moving haul. "We drove all the way down from Portland. I'm Samentha by the way. It's very nice to meet you, Joseph. I'm about ready to collapse, but this one here. . .she's got endless spurts of energy. Her batteries never run low! In fact she could go another two weeks without rest—isn't that right, Nora?"

The girl was clutching Samentha's legs by then, chewing on her mother's t-shirt, and hiding her eyes behind the fabric as if playing a game with me again. Her mother and I continued to talk about her trip and how she already missed the forests, and how she wasn't sure how long it would take for her to get used to the air quality in Los Angeles. But I managed to enchant her with what I found to be the lovelier aspects of where we were— that how, when the clouds would dissipate, one could see all the way to Santa Monica from the balcony. The air was cool that morning, and the flavor of the changing of the seasons was upon us. I had always loved the shades of the afternoon and early evenings where I was living, and I told her that this was one of my favorite things about the building.

Sam had blonde hair that fell to her shoulders, parted in the middle. Her arms were slender, soft, and she kept them wrapped tightly against her body, randomly switching her stance —one knee out, hands on her hips, chewing on her fingernails, giggling at little Nora. She put her hair into a ponytail, then minutes later changed her mind and took out the rubber-band, mentioning something about misplacing her watch at some point on the road. Nora had taken off her pink glasses for a moment, and began to clean them with the bottom of her long orange skirt, saying something about how she couldn't wait to see sunset tonight. Sam agreed that it would be a special evening, but that their beds had not yet arrived and wouldn't for a few days. Then, sweetly and in exhaustion, she gave me a childlike glance, motioning that I look at her daughter. "Now where could my glasses be. . .I thought I had them on my head. My goodness, you little devil. There they are!" Samentha was playing a game of some sorts now, with her daughter.

"No, oh no, Mom, these are *my* glasses! Joseph, she's lying!"

"I don't think so, little one, these are indeed my eyeglasses. I picked them out myself! Pink is my favorite color, because. . . ." Sam stopped and stared back at the child, now squinting playfully up towards her mother.

"Because you and daddy, once upon a time, came across a field of pink roses in a dark, dirty alley. . .when the rain cleared, and I was just a little sparkle in your eyes."

The two kissed softly as they backed up toward the balcony rails, making space for the movers to carry just a few more items into their apartment: a stained-glass window revealing what I could only make out to be a small castle in a forest, which sat below a rising crescent moon; a lamp with a gray shade and an opaque pattern of marching elephants; one love seat, brown, with orange hues; and a large box labeled *Stuffed Animals and Baby Blankets.*

I imagined all of the other silly games that a mother plays with her daughter, wondering of course whether, if Emilie had never touched the bottle, we would have had that chance. To bring up a young mind, to shape their world with a knowledge of music, amidst the shelves in a bookstore or the quiet nights spent looking out the window of our home as a storm moved in. No time for dreaming, Joseph. You might miss an opportunity. Pay attention now.

"But, Mom, look—those are still *my* glasses. Yours are brighter pink! They *are*, Mister Joseph, they are! She's just teasing me because I talked to Daddy this morning, and she doesn't like that."

"Alright now, honey, don't scare the nice man away. You can have your glasses back. Now go and get me something to drink, would you mind? Mommy is parched."

With each word and easy banter, Samentha had an utter calmness to her that I didn't notice right away. Besides, everyone gets nervous when meeting a new neighbor, especially after such a long drive. Perhaps she was in her thirties, but at times it's difficult to tell these things. Her skin was smooth with some acne scars on her forehead. With green eyes to match her daughter's, there was a sadness there I could also sense. Although the way her freckled nose crinkled when she laughed at one of Nora's antics gave me hope. I'd noticed at times, perhaps a premature observation, that Nora's speech seemed much too polite, even neurotic, for such a youngster. Why did this all seem familiar in some way?

Samentha, who are you? A previous student of mine that I had forgotten all about? Where was your husband? She took a small black case from her pocket and put on a pair of glasses, telling me how she had astigmatism in her right eye, and had been thinking about getting contacts but worried about leaving them in too long, mostly on nights when work got much too encompassing for self-maintenance.

It was always exciting when someone new moved in. I do enjoy hearing about the grand adventures that those around me had survived. Endlessly, I fill my quiet hours at home with thoughts like these, the stories that we never do get to hear from a passing stranger. These ideas allow my soul to stir with wonder and curiosity that I imagine no one else would ask for.

When I first came to California, my focus was to forget all about the war in Israel, to just keep playing the piano. For a long while I had been obsessed with the Czech composer Smetana, specifically his tone poems—one I so loved to play was *Má Vlast ("My Homeland")*, a series of six tone poems he had written over the course of half a decade, between 1874 and 1879. I am an admirer of arpeggios.

But I had gotten too carried away in my own thoughts once again, and my two new fireflies were about to leave me, to be on their way, to unpack. To unfurl their tears as well, I imagine, and adjust to a life that would remain theirs for however long they might end up staying in the building. Would they be just as friendly the next time I saw them out on the veranda?

For a second I pictured taking Sam and Nora out for ice cream, when the weather got a little warmer of course. I felt energized, if you don't mind me repeating, by this brief commotion, as if my divorce with Emilie had never taken place, but in the sense that Emilie, in actuality, was no longer a part of my life in a completely new way. But a part of my past, yes, and that was all the thought I was going to give her.

Back to my apartment now. Another Turkish coffee? When was the last time I dusted the keys of my piano? Just the other day, that's right! I had been listening to a new pressing of *The Karasinski & Kataszek Jazz Band*, as there's nothing quite like tending to the maintenance of my piano along to an orchestral tango.

And I will admit, I haven't visited the wintry slopes in a long while. Despite my deplorable injury, I can still manage to get around just fine as an average skier. Have I not mentioned my leg just yet? It's been almost thirty-five years since the accident. There are fragments of that moment I tend to misremember when I tell the story, but in my mind there's not one detail that escapes me. Yours truly, Joseph Brenner, had to jump from a jet plane that suddenly caught fire in the sky. And through that gruesome surge of my body from the plane, and into the cruel atmosphere I endured, some of it I just don't care to think about, since to live through the war is to die a little, and I do not wish this on anyone dear to me. No, not one person. Not even my greatest enemy should know what it's like to get a glimpse of death so intimately.

Although you should know this about me as well: I don't like to use this story as an excuse for anything. You shouldn't feel bad for me, life is not about pity, but circumstance—yes. My body is indeed aging, and despite the impairments I have suffered, I am quite happy, as a man, with blue eyes and a heart that longs to be near others.

And perhaps skiing may not sound so appealing to you, my friend, but I anticipate my trips to the slopes. Of course, with the time it takes to prepare one's gear, and the weather forecast. . .well, these willing aspects are what dictate the possibility of this sort of an excursion. There's a process to everything.

My favorite part is making a list for the trip. It may sound compulsive to you, but preparations are more than necessary in this sport. I bring extra lenses for my goggles, two pairs of ski boots, extra bindings, and my lift tickets. I make copies of the tickets because, if I get robbed on my way from the apartment or my room at the Ambassador, the copies are in the glove compartment of my car.

I wondered if Samentha had ever been skiing. Surely she needed to do something to keep up with her daughter's energy. And why was it that she would leave the enchanting Pacific Northwest to instead inhabit this detached and disruptive city? Los Angeles is a destiny for many people, if they can afford it.

Despite its erratic nature, this beast of a town--there were other elements that I found beneficial, mainly that Los Angeles is a far less traumatic motherland than Israel. For that, I am ever so grateful to inhabit this space. Would I have done it differently? I cannot say, and I most likely never will. I would never have had the opportunity to work as an executive producer at a record company, deep in the heart of Hollywood, if I stayed attached to my time as a pilot. It's difficult to say that I don't have dreams about that glorious day when I first leapt into the sky itself. But the smell of burning oil was not exactly part of the life I had wanted to attain.

You'll also find that I don't identify myself as a sworn Liberal, and yet I am not exactly what you'd call a Republican. It is true that my country has never stopped fighting. The IDF laid down its arms with no apologies. May they never have a chance to escape the illness of that land?

CHAPTER TWO

SUITE 1020

Abigail. Sweet, candid, yet at times subdued. I can still smell her hair on the night we first met: cigarettes, mango, a little red wine. What was it about her that eased me into falling in love again? How could I erase Emilie? I didn't really love her anyhow, not in the way I felt about Abi. It was the way she got up from her table, danced like a gypsy to a Cole Porter ballad. How she clumsily walked over to the bar for another drink, which she would sip slowly, with caution. She came into my life just in time, you could say, in 1978, the year I had my big break, started working for a record company in Hollywood—when the city was just barely surviving off the remnants of what Sinatra had left behind. In his place came Hoffman in *Little Big Man*, an honorable predecessor to Bronson in *Death Wish* I might add. I remember two of the first films I saw in an American movie theater was *Logan's Run*, and then *Deliverance*.

But Abigail wasn't into sci-fi or action movies. She loved a good musical and a comedy that was worth her time.

But I wouldn't have met this woman if it hadn't been for Steve—yes, my dear friend. He was there the night I found her at the Ambassador bar. By day Steve was a law student at Pepperdine. At night he lived out quite a different persona—one his father highly disapproved of. Steve was a piano player, just like me. I had a room at the Ambassador; Steve still lived with his parents in Brentwood. But our connection wasn't just the music. It went a bit further.

"I like how you play. I'm Joseph!" I shouted amid the chaos of the surrounding nightlife. He shook my hand quickly and without much hesitation, took a mighty gulp of what smelled like whiskey, shook his head, and choked for a second.

"You've been playing piano here for a while, I've noticed."

"About a year and a half, actually. Basically gas money for my trips between Brentwood and Malibu."

"I see! And you're a student, I'm judging from your long hair. You've got that look, don't you?"

"Well, yeah, my parents want to kick me out of the house, and this is a surefire way to achieve that by the coming year, after I take the bar exam."

"I wish you luck with your career plans, my friend."

"So what about you, Joseph? Is this where you spend most of your Saturday nights?"

"I will admit, my frequenting this bar has helped me with the divorce."

"Ah, divorced!" he said. "I am sorry to hear that. It's, umm, I'm not even married, so I can't say I understand."

"These are lonely nights but filled with jazz and the hope of finding someone to take home with me. . .look, I'm not in my twenties anymore."

"A few drinks to ease the pain. I know the feeling. I get one or two free at the bar, from playing here. But tell me, what do you do out there in the big bad world?"

"I'm an executive. . .I'm a, uh, an executive producer. At a record company over in Hollywood."

"A music producer!"

"It's not very exciting," I assured him. "Tell me about law school—is it true they put you through the mill?"

"The exams are grueling, truly. The paper chase kills me sometimes, and each time I feel that I'm at the end of my rope, my dad reminds me to tie a knot on the bottom and hang on it a while longer."

"Are you satisfied with that, Steve?"

"I am, to say the least, grateful that he's pushed me to graduate. I am . . .very, very appreciative of that son of a bitch." He leaned in closer to me and started to laugh, raising his eyebrows and downing the rest of his whiskey.

"Steve!" the manager called out from behind the bar. "Dude! Hit the keys. Your break is over, and the dance floor is empty!"

And there he went, perhaps a new friend, a worthy adversary? But by the morning I might forget everything, although I hope that I'll remember all of it—especially what happened next. Just as Steve sat down to the piano, a young brunette slipped onto the seat by my side. "How's your night going so far? Are you so drenched that you've forgot about her, or might you require another round?"

"Forgetting is not the right word," I said. "Celebrating. Yes, celebrating is the right one."

"Oh, but in your eyes I see different story, if I may say so." A witchy yet gently smile appeared on her lips, full, with the tiniest of wrinkles forming around her soft brown eyes. She had a very pleasant-looking face, a small nose turned up slightly in a way that reminded me of a character in a children's book. She appeared empathetic, full of curiosity. I thought, Why me? This hot, unimpressive bar is filled to the brim with gentlemen of all types. Steve was playing a Sinatra melody much to my liking, "The World We Knew."

"Say, stranger," she went on, "do you care to dance?" The slender rose of a woman got up from her chair.

Had I heard her right? Couldn't be. I'm too drunk. And she's much too pretty to have really said that. "What did you just ask me?" I asked in disbelief.

"I wanted to know if you would care to sway with me to some Sinatra."

"I must warn you, I'm not the best dancer." Especially not with my leg injury, but I did want to impress her. Let go, Joseph. At least for tonight. You deserve this. Who am I to resist such a request? Besides, the dance floor was filling up, as if a rush of wind had thrown clumsy bodies onto the stage of a play I had seen a thousand times.

"Well, doll face, this dance is an easy one, I assure you. All you gotta do is hold me and sway along ever so gently. You think you can manage that for the next three minutes?"

"Sure, lady. Sure."

"What did you say your name was?"

"I didn't."

"Okay, your name is *I didn't!* Is that it?" She threw back her head in pure ecstasy, her mouth just so cute I almost couldn't bear to look at it. So I took her outreached hand, and we made our way to the center of the dance floor, which by then was crowded as hell. I put my arms around her. I could feel the cloud of her cashmere sweater she wore so well. And then, I could feel her delicate, firm back as she drew closer to me. And closer now, letting me lead. The music was much too romantic. . .too romantic to resist the moment, and the beer had started to work on me. We swayed into the next song. *This is happening*, I thought. Her perfumed hair touched my cheeks. I felt in control despite the booze, and I so wanted to kiss her, just onto her cheek, that soft and lovely pink cheek. I went in but stopped short, as her hand glided over from my shoulders down to my lower back and back up again, yet this time her palms embraced my neck and she kissed me. *She* kissed *me,* gently. She was far more daring than I could ever be. Was it my lack of confidence, I wondered. . .letting go of control? I wanted to behave like a gentleman, allowing for her to make the first move. But I did, oh yes, I returned the kiss.

"Hey! You two!" Steve called out to us—the song had come to an end. All I could hear was the sound of this feline's heartbeat subdued by my own stubborn will to remain calm and composed after such a kiss. And to my surprise, she seemed to be familiar with Steve, smiling at him now.

"How about another Cole Porter tune, for your tried and true returning customers?" she called back, and once again the music started up, and my new pal Steve was to blame for all of it.

The dance floor continued to fill up with other romantic types. I asked her if she wanted to get a table and order something to eat. She nodded reluctantly but willingly followed me to a corner table. The room was dark, as you might imagine, soft green lamplight shining off the empty glasses, just enough light to conceal the wrinkles and heavily made-up face of the older women who were trying, in vain, to shed a few years from their faces. Outside, where the smokers gathered, it was too bright, more naked, less romantic. But that night it didn't matter much if Abigail went home with me; I just needed some more jazz, a few more drinks, and then I'd head back to my room. This girl couldn't be part of my plan. I just wasn't ready for that sort of thing.

I guess we never are. Abigail spoke up first. "So tell me a bit about yourself, if you like."

I said nothing, frozen by her simple beauty, and it frightened me. She looked a little younger than me, maybe ten years my junior, or thirteen or so. At the table her cheeks looked more rosy and pure, as if she was a young girl, embarrassed after being scolded but withholding any pouting or disappointment with the situation. I could see her better now, and she could see me.

Of course, *Why did I take her to the table? Why not just keep dancing, and kissing—words just get in the way. I am in no shape for this. Why had I come here tonight?* The red wine she was drinking earlier had penetrated her senses, and she was uninhibited.

"Please promise me, Jack, that you won't take advantage of me. I mean Joseph. Sorry."

"You can call me Jack. . .I don't mind."

"Jack. I'm losing control here, and I need to stop drinking for the night, alright? You won't take advantage of me? Promise me."

"It depends on how you use the word 'advantage.' We all look for some advantages in life, don't we? Isn't that why we're both here, tonight, at this fucking sink hole, taking it all in?"

"How far would you go, though?"

"That depends on how strong my opponent is at the moment, but you're in no position to be taken advantage of. . .although you're right, it wouldn't be challenging at all."

"Well, that's quite reassuring to hear, Jack." She was staring at me now. And for a minute we just looked into one another's eyes, in-between songs, a silence that needed no words, no movement, just this. Just *this*.

Then she started to speak once again. "I begin to like you."

"What part of me exactly do you refer to?"

"For one, it's your angular face with the soft green eyes and cleft chin. You remind me of Paul Newman, or Marlon Brando."

"Thanks. That's the best compliment I've heard all month. But will you still like me, tomorrow?"

"You mean when the wine has worn off?"

"Yes!"

"Well, that's a chance you must take, I'm afraid. Are you a gambler in any way?"

"If you consider playing the stock market qualifies, the answer is yes."

And just as I answered her question, I noticed that her head had started to lean a bit to the left. The lady sure wasn't able to hold her alcohol, which meant she might not be a regular drinker. That I liked, a lot. I didn't want to end up with someone like Emilie ever again. In fact, *I* had started drinking perhaps to understand in a way the trauma induced by my life with Emilie and her drinking. I was vigilant to never meet someone like her again, but somehow I had become a bit attached to that terrible habit of my wretched Emilie. It'd only been two years since our divorce, and still I could taste it.

But Abigail seemed, as I've said, a mild case, one who drank occasionally. Or at least I hoped.

We continued to gaze into each other's eyes, as if I could read her mind and she could read mine.

"Jack. . . ?"

"Yes?"

"I feel that you're a very gentle man, with common sense."

"I think I am."

"And while you wouldn't pick a fight, you wouldn't walk away if that was necessary."

"If you mean a fist fight, you're correct. But there are all kinds of fights that happen, some in which I had to be the aggressor. Which I'm not proud of, but that's the life of a man—if you don't stand up for yourself, then you become a victim. Which side do I choose?"

She was looking at me as if she couldn't quite tell what it was I was saying. Or, perhaps she disagreed? "Did you say 'aggressor'?"

"I did."

"I have a hard time picturing you as the aggressor."

"I'm glad you feel that way. And I'm very glad I no longer have to be in that position, since it almost cost me my life. I don't regret my decision to defend myself, though. It was in a good cause."

"What cause was it?"

"A country defending its right to exist."

"That sounds like a vulnerable country, unlike the United States. Am I right?"

"Yes you are. . . . But it's getting late now. And perhaps we should be calling it a day, or shall I say a night."

"Jack, where do you plan on taking me? You *are* taking me *somewhere*, aren't you?"

"Not too far, only ten floors above us."

"Above is a good sign. It means we're taking the high road." She laughed gently. It was nearly 2:00 a.m. I took her hand as we rose from our seats and said our farewells to Steve.

She was silent as we rode the elevator up above the bar at the Ambassador in Mid Wilshire. I took out my key to Suite 1020. Abigail was much too out of it to ask me any more questions, but she did notice my limp as we approached the apartment door. Was she thinking about the "good cause" for which I had defended my country? Or maybe she had to vomit? She could also be on her period, I thought—I should make sure to put a towel down on the bed for her just in case.

I wasn't going to seduce her. No, nothing like that. It was clear there was an attraction. The booze helped, but it wasn't just plainly being under the spell of alcohol. I was under *her* spell, in fact, but I wouldn't let her know it just yet.

The suite contained one bedroom, a kitchenette, and a small, cozy den where I often fell asleep reading the paper late at night. As you entered, you could smell the obvious hotel aroma. The den had a small table with artificial flowers in a gold-plated vase. Two armchairs and a love seat filled the remainder of the space, and a fifty-two-inch television set hung from the wall.

I kept my bedroom dimly lit. Abigail sank onto the queen-sized bed and was sound asleep the second she hit the pillow. I removed her heels very gently and covered her with an extra blanket that I fetched from the walk-in closet. I watched her sleep for a few minutes, wondering what she was dreaming about, and whether maybe by chance of me. I crashed on the love seat for what was left of the night. . .a few short hours. I couldn't be sure of her name, though; had she told me and I forgot? I did remember to remove my shoes, but I didn't use the bathroom. I'd be up in a few hours to do so.

Morning came. We slept until around noon. The young woman opened her eyes and seemed a bit confused about where she was. But I watched quietly, from my love seat, as she picked up the menu by the side of my bed. Maybe she realized where she was—and at the Ambassador no less. She found me eventually, complained about a slight hangover, and we slowly reminisced about the sequence of events that had taken place the night before.

When she stared at me for a few seconds, I could tell she couldn't remember my name, but it came to her eventually. "Jack, is it?"

"Yes."

"Oh, I was so worried I'd forgotten your name!"

"Well, it's Joseph. But you can call me anything you like."

"How handsome you are in the full light of the morning, Jack," she said as I watched her body move closer to the soft sunlight of late November falling through the wooden shutters, illuminating my face. I could see that she wasn't sorry for anything she had done up until now.

Quickly though, she ran off to the bathroom. I rose from the love seat and looked around the den, wondering if I should rush to make us some coffee, a bit uncertain about what I would say to her when she came back from the bathroom.

But it was I who didn't know *her* name—she already knew me as Joseph and "Jack," and I giggled at the thought that she had chosen a new name for me.

She came into view with her hair partially covering her right eye, dark eye-liner smudged on her left, and a very shy look on her face as if she was asking me, *How the fuck did all this happen so quickly. . .so spontaneously?*

But before I could make sense of any of these things, I had to have a cup of coffee. I smiled at her, unapologetically but without any regrets. I was just happy to see such a sight—this mysterious woman standing in the broad morning light. She was so cute and intelligent.

"Did you. . .umm, take advantage of me last night, when I passed out in your bed?"

"I already told you that taking advantage over a helpless person is no challenge for me."

I don't know why I kept referring to this idea. It falls short; it's much too protective. Besides, if I didn't want her I wouldn't have brought her back with me. I don't know who I was kidding. But I had my doubts. I was sure she had a boyfriend, or an entire slew of men just waiting for her to make herself available. A woman like that knows how to play with one's heart.

"Did you sleep in the other room the entire night?"

"The whole night, in the den. Although the whole night wasn't so whole!"

"Yes, that's true! Geez, what time did we make it back to your place?"

"Around 2:00, we came upstairs. . . . I could hear you from the den."

"You heard me? Doing what?" she asked, blushing like the sun setting in the mid-West after a snowstorm.

"I heard you snoring, my dear, like a toad!"

"Well, what a start, what a mighty embarrassing interlude we've had so far, don't you think?" she countered, a creature of many delights.

But would she have me? Maybe not this afternoon, but another time we could meet up. Although, I couldn't be sure I'd be so readily available for a woman of such foxiness. She was sublime.

"How about we go downstairs for some breakfast," she said. "On me . . .we'll exchange numbers there. But before I forget, I'm Abigail, Abi for short." And she glided toward the front door, waiting for me to follow her lead.

I almost didn't, but then I asked myself, Why not find out what's next? So I grabbed my wallet and tossed her my keys. "You can lock up behind us. I'm going to run down to the mailroom. I'll see you for breakfast in ten," I added, though I wouldn't usually be so trusting with something like keys to my home, in the hands of a strange woman.

I guess you can say a man like me often hesitates in such a situation—when I'm not exactly in control. But I'd already started on my way to the mailroom. I passed the mirrored hallway where the second elevator was, and realized how tired I looked. But so did Abi. And to tell you the truth, I hate to leave my hotel without first washing up and changing my clothes. But there was no one in the mailroom. Any normal socialite is at work. I've got to get back into a schedule. Just some junk mail, and something from my doctor.

Alright then, Joseph. It's time for breakfast, which means I have to talk to Abi without the spell of booze between us. I'm coming to you, my lady. I'm coming.

I took the long way, back around to the other side of the complex, cordially greeting a few residents. Some looked like they'd survived some drastic circumstances of their own, with eyes that burned holes into my own fears. Others strolled by with their noses in the air, arms folded clumsily across their chests, humming some god-awful disco tune under their breath.

"Jack! Over here!"

"It's *Joseph*, ya know."

"Oh, my goodness, you're right. . .you're right. Joseph. Join me! Here, sit across from me. Did you want to start with a coffee?"

"Well, I was thinking—"

"I personally don't take part in the ingestion of many stimulants," she said. "Even last night was something rare for me. I have a drink maybe once a month or so." She was a bit nervous, I could tell, but also fresh in her composure. I tried not to stare too deeply into her eyes. The wallpaper was peeling above us, and down the strip of tables came our dumpy waitress, with purple lipstick to match her skirt and suspenders.

"Whaddaya want, kids? Looks like you two could use some breakfast . . .well, you've got about an hour until the cook moves on to lunch, so it's your call. Our special today is the blackberry crepes, two for 89 cents. Coffee's on the house for veterans."

"Joseph, would you like to lead?"

"Sure, I'll have a large coffee, black, sugar on the side, three lumps if you please. And I'll take two orders of the crepes, and some hash browns. And, I am, umm, a veteran."

"Ah, I see. I thought you looked a little too well-composed for a man in his thirties. Those military men, they sure do know how to put together an outfit. And for you, honey?"

"I'll take the. . .side of coleslaw, and fruit if you have any in season. No coffee for me, I'd instead like a warm water with fresh lemon—squeezed or on the side. And a stack of your flapjacks. You don't have some of that luscious chocolate syrup and whipped creme do you?"

"And the works for the lady. I'll bring your drinks in a minute." The elephant stomped off into her jungle clanking with silverware and steaming pots of caffeine as Happy Couples bickered at their tables or ignored one another staring off out the window. One kid, about twelve or so, was pacing the aisles between us and the kitchen, chewing on what appeared to be a very large pickle.

"Why are children so disgusting, Joseph?" Abi asked, twirling her fingers into a pile of sugar she poured onto our table.

"I don't think they're so terrible. I plan to have some children one day."

"Oh? Is that so?"

"It's never too late to start a family. I just gotta find a girl."

"Yeah, a nice girl is hard to find. You miss your ex-wife?"

"Not in the slightest."

"So tell me, porcupine heart, you're a veteran? When we left the dance floor to head upstairs, I thought I noticed a slight limp."

"You were quite observant, in spite of the wine running through your veins last night."

"Will you tell me the story, Jack, behind my drunken surveillance?" As she finished her sentence I stood up and took a walk in front of our table, allowing my limp to show to the max. "This is what happens," I began, "when you jump off a burning fighter jet ten thousand feet above ground and don't land exactly the way they taught you in boot camp. My plane was shot down over the Suez Canal in October 1973." I sat back down at the table, and our waitress brought our drinks.

I stared at mine for a few seconds, until she asked, "So who shot you down?"

"The Egyptians, during a bombing mission. I managed to reach the ground after having been ejected. I fractured my leg in four places. The doctors gave me a very, very small chance of ever walking again on this leg.... But here I am, like a fool having accepted your invitation to dance. A woman in front of me. A woman with a face I couldn't say no to."

"Oh, Joseph! Please don't do this. Tell me you're only kidding and that I didn't cause you any unnecessary pain last night. If I'd known, I wouldn't have—"

"Don't. Enough feeling sorry for yourself. After all, the injury belongs to me. I can deal with it. Besides, I'm fine now. Seriously."

"Did you return from the U.S. that October, to fly again for the Israeli Air Force?"

"I did. I was called back and asked if I could jump onto the next flight to Tel Aviv. The country was being attacked from three directions. I didn't have much time to spare. But if you must know. . .I was in the middle of my MBA studies, over in Northridge, when I was called back. And my girlfriend didn't like it a bit—no, not a bit. She called every night to check if I was still upright, if I was still aboveground. At the time she and I were planning our wedding. Perhaps that's why the marriage didn't work out. I don't know at this point."

When I finally shut the hell up, Abi looked at me in the face for a long while. We shared a smile or two, and our breakfast was placed in front of us. I could see her blood-shot eyes, but it didn't matter much to me: She was beautiful. A lovely woman sat across from me. I could feel her warmth, and I finally let it in. I could see she wanted to say something but wasn't sure of where to direct our conversation next. I wanted to ask about her younger years, but before I could get a word out I started to reminisce about the night before. She could have called a cab, or asked me to call one for her. Why take a chance on a stranger? Why did she want me?

. . .*Is he for real?* I imagined her thinking. She didn't want to fall again, and so quickly, for a man. She was getting too old for it.

"So, Joseph!" she began abruptly, and then stopped.

"What's going on in that head of yours, darling? Talk to me."

"May I ask you another personal question?" she said, and I smiled to confirm. ". . .Well, I was just curious why you reserved that suite last night?"

"Actually, I didn't have to reserve it. It's sort of my home."

"I *thought* it looked lived in. . .but who lives in a hotel these days? It's so rebellious of you. Doesn't that get expensive?"

"My father was owed a pretty penny, a large loan if you will, by one of the stockholders here at the Ambassador. You could say the debt, which was eventually paid to him, became my road to freedom after my divorce from Emilie in 1977. The agreement allows for me to reside at unit 1020 for the remainder of my life. They gave my father the right to the suite, which ends when I die. After the divorce two years back, I came here, and I've been here ever since. Beverly Hills is home, and I can't complain. But it's much too small for me, although I do appreciate the coziness of a bachelor's pad. I'm the only one who has access to the suite. I'll move out eventually and buy a condo in Mid Wilshire."

"So you'll have two places, then? How fascinating. And you must do well, if you can purchase a condo."

"I do well in my field. It gets exhausting, but I'm grateful." We smiled and watched a new waiter approach us, probably the shift change for lunch. He was an older man, skinny as a pole, with graying hair and a red towel wrapped around his right hand. He wore a white jacket embroidered with the letters *A.H.*, much more appropriate than the waitress who had served us before dressed like a streetwalker.

"Hello, my friends," he said. "As you may already have been told, we're nearing our lunch hour, so in about twenty-five minutes breakfast will no longer be served. Would you like anything off the menu before we do the switch?" he added hurriedly.

Abi got a devilish look on her face and nodded to me. "That sounds like a good idea, darling," said I. "May I order for us?"

"Why not?"

I turned to the waiter. "We'll take an order of waffles, four eggs over medium, link sausage with maple syrup on the side, whole-wheat rolls with butter, and another coffee for me."

Just as I trailed off, Abigail quickly rose from the table and ran toward the ladies room. Perhaps she'd seen her reflection in the window and decided to powder her nose? She hadn't showered or anything yet, and maybe she'd realized how she had left her bra on my bed and was embarrassed?

. . .How did I miscalculate? The second month in a row that my period arrived three days late. Maybe I need to see my OB-GYN*? I was a bit depressed this last week. That often disrupts my cycle. And then a night of drinking into the morning. . . . I should have been more prepared. Luckily I always keep some extra tampons in my bag. God, I hope he doesn't think I'm a loony, some unkept girl who can't keep track of her period. Did I bleed through? Did. . .oh, Lord. No, I'm in the clear. No stains, but no bra. . .where did I leave it?*

By the time Abi returned to our table, the waiter had brought our whole-wheat rolls. We feasted on those for a few minutes, and I asked her if she was feeling alright. "Can I be of any help? You seem a little distraught, if you don't mind my noticing."

"Oh, it's just a girly thing, really. I'm fine. I didn't realize I had somehow misplaced my. . .well—" she leaned in to whisper to me— "my bra . . .I've misplaced my bra. Do you find me completely disgusting?"

"Not at all. Your secret's safe with me."

"*Thank* you, Jack," she said, laughing to herself, saying my new name over and over again: "Jack, Jack, Jack."

Then she looked at my hands, grabbed my wrist, and read the time out loud. "Oh! I feel like I haven't showered in months."

"Yeah, I'm feeling kind of full already, too. I don't know what we were thinking with the second breakfast. Once the rest of our food arrives, let's pack it up. I'll drive you home, and we can return to our previous lives."

"Previous lives? What do you mean? In my previous life, I would have never danced with a stranger, especially not one who jumped out of a burning fighter jet and lived to tell the tale. So you're saying that you'd like to move on from me, then? Is that it? I see your logic. . .one which doesn't include me?"

"Oh, it includes you. Yes. If you'd. . .if you'd like to be included."

"I can live with that for now."

"But before we go, won't you tell me a little about your own life? I have to have something more to go on in case you do decide to see me again."

"I married young and got divorced four years later. I'm the branch manager at a nearby bank, where I supervise twenty-three employees. And they aren't the worst bunch of folks, roughly in their early twenties. A few are up there, in their sixties. I just turned thirty-two, so that makes me twenty-five when I wed. No children, as Tom—that's my ex; he had a low sperm count and, well, he refused to try any treatments. But that wasn't the reason for our divorce. When I first met him, he was a customer at the bank. I fell for his good looks, and he was a true gentleman. He had brain on him for sure. When we fell for each other he was finishing some psychology classes, so it would have been another year until he'd obtain his MFCC license. But as I know much too well. . .that never materialized, and he became a highly educated unemployed young man."

"Sounds awful. And you didn't want to wait around, it sounds like?"

"I grew weary. I was just so tired of supporting him. And after a while his temper started getting out of control. One morning, after I had finished doing the bills and put on a little make-up, I was making my way out the front door to work when Tom asked me for some money, but I didn't have any extra cash on me that day. He hit me. Right in the face. And I never saw him again after that."

Abi suddenly blushed again and grew quiet, as if holding in a deep sob coming through to the surface. Should I tell her about my ex-wife the drunk? Now would be the time. The waiter brought the rest of our food, and Abigail packed everything up nicely in our to-go boxes, humming a familiar song under her breath. We took the elevator down to the parking lot, as the attendant pulled up in a black BMW sedan, opened the door for Abi. Opened my door as well.

"Where to, dear Abigail?"

"I'm on Coldwater Canyon Boulevard, just north of Melrose."

"Not too far from here! Just a few miles, actually."

We arrived at the front of a two-story house with a lovely front yard framed by maple trees and palms of all sizes. She got out of my car and paced a few times around the semi-circular driveway, and I watched her for a minute. She glanced my way, then got shy and continued to pace.

"So this is you, then?"

"Yes! This is my humble little castle I like to call home. Thanks to my parents' generosity—they put down twenty percent."

"It's immaculate. Truly, just breathtaking. Do you do all this gardening yourself?"

"When I get a day off work, I like to be out in the sunshine, collecting ladybugs and aphids on my brow."

"Tell me, before I go, what is it you plan to do with the rest of your life? Just so I can get an idea, you know. My job gets tedious, and sometimes it's nice to know what other people get up to. With their future."

Joseph, I was thinking, just get back in your goddamnn car and leave, get out of here. You're no good for her, she's much too special. I'd just spoil her life.

"Well, Jack," she said, "what I do with the rest of my life depends on . . .it depends on you." She was close to me now, and I could smell the sweet maple syrup on her breath. But I couldn't say a word back, and so she led the way. As she tends to do so nicely. "Whaddaya say? I'd love to go out with you later this week, and hopefully the week after that. And, maybe, if you like me. . .for the months to follow."

I didn't kiss her, no. I should have, but I didn't. We embraced for a few seconds, I could feel her heartbeat, and it was steady. Suddenly I was watching her disappear from behind the front door, into her house. I wondered if she had a cat, perhaps a tabby?

CHAPTER 3

VANILLA AND STRAWBERRY ICE CREAM

The temperature at that time of the day felt like a miracle. Swarms of yellow warblers and cedar waxwings filled the inner greenscapes of the trees indigenous to Los Angeles. The laurel sumac was often one of my most admirable specimens. In front of Beverly Gardens, you can sit below one of the largest Morton Bay fig trees in the area. And although this tree was quite a sight, it had its own imperfections, much like you and I. In my pocket I kept a few juniper berries from my walk earlier, although I couldn't tell you why. Intuition? A new habit to keep my mind busy, when otherwise I'd be lamenting to myself.

Sometimes I pass a store front and catch my reflection. For a moment I look like a boy, eager for the simpler things in life: riding my bike to the market, not yet aware of what words like 'intuition' or 'indifference' mean. I will say to you that I am appreciative of my life as it stands now. But I am still that boy, curious, inventive, my girlfriend has mentioned to me here and there. I am still that boy, just tucked inside a body that maintains its progress.

I could hear Steve coming up to my apartment. There's something very specific that sets his arrival apart from anyone else's—he is always humming out loud to whatever piano piece we've most recently been working on, his voice now a bit more frail than when I met him years back. Yet I hear his voice echoing through the stairwell, and I start singing along.

But at that moment, Steve was no longer meeting me for a late night at the Ambassador bar. Steve, my alter ego? Not so much, although I do cherish my forties more than any other decade along this stubborn timeline. I noticed recently that my comrade had sprouted a few gray hairs on his sideburns, and even that his hair's thinning—a slight receding above his forehead. Oh, it comes.

Steve has been a reluctantly successful junior partner at a well-respected law firm, specializing in workmen's compensation cases. His father carved his path, and ever since he's given up playing the piano at our lovely bar. Still, it's true that, after eighteen years, Steve has remained one of my very closest friends. That being said, I was nervous about seeing him, because more than anything I wanted to tell him about Samentha and Eleanor. Earlier this morning, I brought Sam a cup of my sterling Turkish coffee, and for Nora a pink scarf that my grandmother had once given to my mother, when she was a child. Pink of course, to match Nora's glasses. We had a short encounter, but it was enough to fill my day with a bit more joy than I'm accustomed to.

As soon as Steve reached my door, he went straight to my piano to play Sinatra's "My Way." It was often how we warmed up for a session, and I could tell he was ready to burst with musical delight.

I mentioned something about the new neighbors but didn't go into too many details. I don't wish to get carried away with my newfound fascination. And it's hard to explain exactly what about the feeling is all-encompassing. It was as if I knew Eleanor already. Do you know that feeling when you meet someone, and they remind you of what's been missing from your life? Steve would probably tell me that I was ruminating too deeply over my regrets for not having a child.

So I spent most of my day recollecting when I'd first met Abi. And not just our chance meeting eighteen years ago, but why it was we didn't start a family together.

After making it halfway through the song, Steve looked at me and began with his questions, as he tends to do when we first meet up.

"Joseph, hey now, isn't Abigail coming back into town this evening?"

"You're wrong, my friend—she's still out of town, about another week or so. Monday she'll return. I'm to pick her up around 4:30."

"You miss her terribly, don't you?"

"I always do."

"So, then, it's just us tonight?"

"I'm afraid so."

"Well, I'm famished. Did you call in dinner?"

"Indeed I did. It should arrive any minute."

"You're a genius. Alright, so. . . ." He started to play around on my piano with more zest now: A nice waltz carries the conversation well.

". . .So you've got these new neighbors you said? You're in the midst of a whole new set of energies, a young woman and her daughter. Who knows, maybe you've met the girl of *my* dreams."

"I don't know much about her husband, though, or if she even has one. I haven't noticed a man around yet. But women are more solo runners these days, you can't just show up and expect to make her swoon."

"I dunno, Joseph, Abi's not always present herself at your place, so how can you make such a judgement? Maybe she's got a husband, and he travels around. I don't want to be that 'other man'. Besides, Kathy and I are. . . ."

"What's going on between you two?"

"Let's not spoil our night together. Tell me, is this Samentha cute? And, what's her daughter like? I can handle a kid—come on, don't look at me with that face of conviction!" Steve exclaimed.

"You should know this woman's got a good head on her shoulders, and her daughter, Eleanor, she's very bright. A bit neurotic for her age, though."

"Kids are weird in general. I could see you possibly being neurotic as a child. Not terribly unusual. So is Sam cute or what?!"

"As a matter of fact, she's *very* cute, about your height, maybe an inch or two shorter. Which means that, if you do take her out, no high heels for her. What are you, five-eight now?" I didn't intend to insult him, but sometimes he asks for it.

"Give me a break, I'm not shrinking just yet. I'm still five-ten."

"Alright then, I'm going to get some more coffee ready for us, if you don't mind. Will you be a good boy and listen for the—"

The doorbell cut me off, and Steve was much too busy pulling out notes for our session from his backpack. I rushed to the door, took hold of our takeout bags, and asked Steve if he had any small bills for the tip. All I had was a five-dollar bill left over from my change. Could be a substantial amount to offer the young delivery guy. He didn't seem too well off himself, but while running around town amid a hundred deliveries, one might appear more disheveled than usual.

As I was closing the door, I glanced at Samentha's door, and just as I was about to turn away I saw Eleanor's tiny face pop out, smiling in my direction.

"Ahoy there, Elie. How are you this evening?"

"I'm fine, sir, just fine. I couldn't help but smell something delicious. . . ."

"We've just ordered in some Chinese food! Might you and your mother be *ravenously* hungry?" I called out with perhaps too much excitement.

Young Eleanor nodded and ran right up to my door. And there she was.

I felt my anxiety suddenly dissipate. "Listen, dear, if the two of you like, come in for a bite to eat. I also have some snacks."

"Do you mean *ice cream?*" the child whispered as she looked side-to-side, making sure her mother didn't hear what she had just confessed.

"There is a *slight* chance that I have some ice cream."

"Mom! Mama! The man asked if we would come and eat with him! There's ice cream, too!"

"What man?" said Samentha as she walked onto the balcony, distracted by a phone call. "Honey, I'm busy with Granny right now. You know our phone calls are very important. More important than ice cream."

"What could be more important than ice cream, right, Nora?" I couldn't help myself. I should have said that good girls always listen to their mothers.

"Mom! What's more important than ice cream? Tell Granny we have to go. We have to go eat ice cream *now!*" the child shouted toward the telephone at Sam's ear, pulling down on her mother's elbow, throwing a small fit yet not lingering for too long. Sam turned toward her apartment and continued to talk with her mother, disappearing back into her own apartment. "Mama, I've got to tend to Nora over here, it's way past her dinnertime. . .no, they haven't delivered our beds just yet. Mama, I've tracked the bed, and it's on its way, but we've been sharing the couch. . . . It's actually kind of fun in a way, like we're camping without all the nasty pests. . . . Mm-hm, yes, Mama." Sam waved her hand goodbye in my direction, and closed her door. But little Nora had stayed close by.

"Mom is on the phone, sir."

"Okay. Well, you can tell her that the two of you are still invited, and we'll wait for you."

"Who is 'we,' sir?"

"Oh. My very good friend Steve. I'll introduce you two shortly. I guarantee you'll both like him."

"But my mom told me I can't like strangers, didn't I tell you?"

Another process I tend to enjoy is preparing a table. Not everyone is lucky enough to have friends, alive and well, to share a meal beside. These things I think about often. So I began to open up the packaged food, the sounds of the Styrofoam rubbing against the plastic cutlery I rather like. Very slowly I lay everything out onto the dining room table, along with some paper plates, forks and knives, and of course some cups--glass, though. One must always drink out of glass cups.

Steve was finishing up a few ballads while I finally made my way into the kitchen to get the coffee brewing. Suddenly, I heard a bit of a commotion, in the living room perhaps, but wondered, who is Steve talking to, though? Surely not to himself, that's just not like him.

"Oh, hello there. I'm Joseph's partner in crime, Steve. And you're... let me guess, the new neighbors he's been carrying on about?"

"Steve, it's a pleasure. This is my daughter Eleanor, and I'm Samentha."

"Hi there, Eleanor—I like your glasses. Won't you both come inside?"

"Was that you playing the piano earlier?"

"Yes, it was, although Joseph also plays."

"I'd like for Eleanor to take some lessons. Something I never had the opportunity to do as a child." Sam brushed out her daughter's hair with her fingers, then making her tiny baseball cap crooked, one crocheted with butterflies on black cotton canvas.

"Where'd you grow up, Samentha?" Steve asked.

"In the city—well, Culver City more specifically."

"Did you go to high school locally?"

"Hamilton High, Go Tigers," she unenthusiastically replied.

"No kidding! Wait, I was there! I was at Hamilton High, well, in the Eighties."

"Oh, yeah?" she said, blushing.

"Did you go to college as well? Not that it matters. I mean, if you didn't, I wouldn't think any less of you." Steve began to get nervous (it was obvious), and Samentha was pleased.

"I did go to college," she said. "I finished at UCLA in their nursing program, and from there I went to work for a Children's Hospital out here in Los Angeles. After some time, Mama wanted to make a big move. So off to Oregon I went."

"Oregon is quite a place."

"Well, Mama made the leap, so I decided I'd follow her after Nora was born. . . . Honey why don't you go and see if Joseph needs help in the kitchen."

"Is it just the one child?" Steve inquired a bit under his breath.

"Oh, no! I'm sorry, I call Eleanor by Nora at times. Maybe I'm just lazy."

"Nora is a lovely name. It really is."

"Do you have any children, Steve?"

"Me? No, not *yet,* though. I had been planning on starting a family next year, but things have been changing recently."

"With your wife?"

"I wouldn't exactly call her my wife. . . ."

"Oh. I see. Well, at least you don't have to worry about a kid, not to say I'm anyone's hero—but it's not easy being a single mom. You'll meet someone else."

"So tell me, why did you leave Oregon?" Steve had to pry.

"I can't say that my leaving Oregon was planned. Everything sort of fell apart. John—my husband—his parents were also living in Oregon at that time. So in the beginning we were able to merge both our families, something that not every couple gets a chance to do. And for that while, everything was perfect. And John himself was from Oregon, so it worked out nicely. He knew everyone there."

"I'm sorry, did you say that your husband. . .that he *was* from Oregon?"

"Yes. Was. John passed away some three years ago. He was killed in an air crash. . . . What a way to break the ice, huh? I guess we should have a drink first before we begin the whole regrets conversation."

"Oh, don't even worry, Samentha. I'm so sorry for your loss. Was he a passenger?"

"Oh, no. John flew private corporation jets on company flights around the country. But at times he would fly to the Far East as well."

"He was away most of the time, I imagine?"

"Yes, he was. Always so far away. Nora didn't like that one bit at all, and I never did adjust to his long absences either. But he loved his work, and his wages were quite substantial. Either way, here we are." She looked down for a minute, sort of fussing with her tennis shoes. I could see Steve was working his magic on her from the kitchen, and I hoped he was being a gentleman. Perhaps it was time I checked in.

"Is this true, Samentha? I'm so sad to hear about your husband. Flying is a dangerous business alright, especially when missiles are chasing after you," I said to her, with respect but at the same time I slipped and made it about my own experience as a pilot—which I tend to do, if you haven't noticed already.

"You have a bit of an accent, don't you, Joseph?" she asked.

"Perhaps! But no matter, I wanted to say how blessed we are to have both you and Nora for dinner. There's nothing like sharing a meal. Food's almost ready! I just need to finish a few more things here. Steve, can you come and help me real quick?"

"Yeah, yeah—I'm busy, Jack!"

"No one calls me Jack but my Abi!" I hollered back to Steve as I made my way into the kitchen.

"Who's this Abi?" Samentha wanted to know.

"Abigail is Joseph's girlfriend. We all met on the same night, eighteen years ago. He's sort of been like a father to me. My own dad is a good man, but we just don't have much in common. We especially don't share the same love for music, the way Joseph and I do."

"Joseph has a kindness about him, doesn't he?"

"Yeah. He's got a lot of heart. And I'm still as smitten as I was the first day we played music together," Steve reminisced. He was feeling comfortable with her, as if they were old friends catching up.

"I never met my father. But mama used to tell me bits and pieces about him."

"When did he pass?" he asked.

"All I know is that he was a pilot in the Israeli Air Force. It's no wonder I ended up marrying a pilot."

"Would you ever remarry? I mean, granted that's a lot to think about when you've got the kid around."

"Maybe I'll marry again. Or, maybe I won't. So what's *your* life story, under ninety seconds?"

"Under ninety seconds? Are you crazy?"

"Come on, I bet you could do it."

"Well, okay. . .maybe there's not so much to tell. I too graduated from UCLA, and then moved on to study at Pepperdine's School of Law—not my choice, really my father's influence—but I have been practicing law now for a few years. As you know I do play the piano, she is my mistress, but I used to play professionally. Not so much anymore. That's when I met Joseph, at the Ambassador bar."

"Eighteen years ago!"

"Yes, exactly. . .and that's where he met Abigail. It was a few years after his divorce. Reluctantly, he was ready for the real thing. His ex, whom I never met but heard awful stories about, was quite selfish. Heavy drinker. Shut him out of her life. He doesn't like to talk much about her."

Steve paused for a second, and suddenly they both stopped talking.

Why? Aside from running the garbage disposal and pouring the drinks, I was unable to focus really on any decipherable words between the two. As long as Steve wasn't chasing her away. *Well, Joseph,* I told myself, *it's time to serve your guests.* I made my way into the dining room, where they sat together awaiting the next stage of our evening together.

"And now, everyone. . .let's eat!" I said to my company.

"Can I have my vanilla and strawberry ice cream now?" shouted wild-eyed Eleanor, leaning most of her body over the table and reaching out with her tiny hands in my direction. Samentha calmed her down, making sure she waited patiently.

"Who wants egg rolls?" I called out.

"Me! I do!" the girl exclaimed.

"Nora, we must make a better impression," Samentha insisted.

"Elie, you can have your ice cream when your mother says so, but first you'll have some egg rolls. Okay? And do you know when your refrigerator arrives? I can bring over some ice cream then, as well." I figured it was best I let her mother lead. I could spoil Nora another time.

"Tomorrow by noon—that's when our refrigerator comes!" Eleanor screamed out. She was something, alright. After inhaling her rice and egg rolls, I set her up in the living room with some children's programming on the television and a small plate with two heaping mounds of vanilla and strawberry delight. Once I returned to the dining room, Sam and I got to talking some more. She had to catch me up on what I'd missed while I was in the kitchen. Steve adored her already, I could see it in the uncomfortable way he was sitting in his chair, so stiff, and much too attentive. But that was part of his charm.

"You said your husband was a pilot?" I asked her.

"John was in the air force when we met, and by the time we got married he was still in the service. I was thirty-two when Nora was born. She's turning eight next February." Furtively, Steve and I did the math in our heads regarding Sam's age.

"Your mother's still up in Oregon, you were telling me?" Steve said.

"She would have been sixty today, but no. . .she passed right before John's fatal accident. I was devastated. The worst part is, if you don't mind my elaborating—"

"Yes, do," I said, pouring her another glass of sparkling water.

"The worst part is that. . .that I don't even *know* if I'm an orphan myself, since I never met my biological father. Mama only married once, to a man named Jim. They were married when I was two years old, but it ended. I. . .I was around five when they split up, and I have very little recollection of him."

"This is quite a story," I said out loud. Why couldn't I have just kept that inside? I stood up and stretched, asked if anyone needed another cup of my Turkish coffee, but got no bites. Nora had come into the dining room; she was finished with her cartoons, her face and t-shirt covered in ice cream.

Then Samentha spoke up, looking much more relaxed. "Steve, would you play a song for me before we leave for the night?"

"Sure. It would be an honor." He fumbled out of his chair, grabbing the bottle of wine to empty into his glass. He offered to pour Samentha some as well, and she quickly downed the sparkling water so that he could refill it with the sweet red vino. "Do you have a song in mind, one that you'd like me to play?"

"'Don't Let the Sun Go Down,' by Elton John, if you know it—maybe it's an impossible request," she added, smiling playfully at him. And she watched him make his way to my piano. He sat down, took a deep breath, and looked up to the ceiling, running his fingers up and down the scales, louder and then softer, mesmerizing both Samentha and me. We closed our eyes. She had told me earlier that she still felt tired. Yet during our night together, her green eyes shone in the softly lit dining room. Her blonde hair was pulled back by a single black ribbon. I opened one eye to look at her and could see that she was still in Steve's trance, waiting for the first line of the song to appear.

Steve began glancing back at her, thinking (I guessed) how cute she was, and that he'd better not mess up the song.

And he was thinking that she was about his age, and that she wouldn't be interested in me, would she? I was twenty years older than Sam and tied up, Steve knew, with Abigail. *So that leaves just me,* he concluded, *and, I must ask her out to dinner before she meets another guy. But not tonight, no that's too soon. Not tonight.*

Samentha appeared deep in thought herself. At first it was the music that carried her into momentary bliss, but soon I could tell, from the way she was looking at him, that she was thinking many things, perhaps wondering if Steve was as handsome as John had been. On the other hand, she'd always wanted to date a piano player. There was something so intriguing on that level, that passion, that drive to create something. . . .

But the night had to come to an end. The child looked tired—little Nora muttering that her batteries were running low and that sleep was coming, oh yes, sleep, the place where dreams are born. As Sam and her daughter made their way to the front door, Steve was already waiting for them with his kind smile and his childlike demeanor. The two adults conducted a bit more conversation—on how Nora had been enrolled at a small school in Beverly Hills three weeks back, which was luckily just a few miles away. Samentha thanked us both graciously for "feeding these two hungry females!" as she put it. And then they left.

Steve and I cleared the table, and he revealed to me that he'd have to move fast with Samentha, while she was still new to the area. He could show her around, and they could get to know each other better. I asked him, though, about Kathy—their last big argument had been about career differences.

"Complications have been dragging along for a long while now, Joseph. I'm just sorry I didn't come to you when our issues first came to the surface. I wanted to maintain that stature, you can say, I guess, to stand in my power. I didn't want to admit it, but Kathy and I just can't cut it together."

"What happened?"

"Can we sit down for a minute?" he asked, and we made ourselves comfortable. "Look," he said, "Kathy's applying to an in-class masters program out of state."

"Out of state?"

"Yeah. And I can't change her mind. I take it to mean that she's done with the relationship. I asked her if she could also apply to some local programs, but she refused. The only option she gave me was that we try a long-distance relationship for the two years—but no, man. No way. We both know that, once a few months go by, it's over. Love doesn't work that way. It doesn't stretch that far beyond the boundaries of hope. Love is never that pure or that patient."

". . .You're probably right," I said after reflecting on it. "I'm sorry about Kathy. You alright? I mean, you feel good about this? Sure you don't want to check out this out-of-state school with her?"

"Joseph, Kathy's thirty-five, and her biological clock is ticking away. I'm gonna be forty next month, and I don't want to wait another two years to start a family. I can't do the waiting game. Not for me." He got up and started to remove the dirty napkins from the dining room table, and the scraps of food, and stacking it all into a pile.

"Looks like we'll need another garbage bag," he said. Want me to grab it?"

"Not just yet. Now, look. . .I like Kathy. I do."

"You don't have to sympathize with her end of things. Really, it's over, Joseph. We've both decided—well, we just left it at that last conversation and haven't exactly *said* it's over. But who wants to say those words out loud?"

"When's her program scheduled to start?" I asked, moving the salt and pepper shakers around and fixing my hair in the mirror behind him.

"By January she'll be in Denver. I guess it's not *terribly* far. . . ."

"Her career is important to her, so for her it's worth the sacrifice is what it sounds like, if you don't mind my saying so. She may even be disappointed you can't see it in that light."

"I suppose I'm more old-fashioned. I want my goddess to have the career she desires, but I want a wife who's a devoted mother and accommodating, with a lopsided division of labor!"

"Oh, Steve, listen to what you're saying. That arrangement may have worked in your parents' generation, so I am afraid you may just stay a professional bachelor for a while longer. And Samentha is a single mother and a career-driven woman, too. She's quite capable of taking care of herself and Eleanor. I don't believe that she's searching for a man who'd expect her to stay home. I think she may even bring in a hundred twenty-five thousand a year."

". . .You think? That's umm, that's a nice number." Steve gulped, then continued, "No, you're right. I've got my head in the clouds. She moved here for upward mobility, for opportunities, and she'll continue to advance her economic prospects."

"Steve, do you see yourself accepting a woman of such radiance? You feel threatened by her, don't you."

"Well, intrigued anyway. But yes, perhaps slightly threatened. . .I think a lot about my mom, her role as a mother and a wife first. She stayed home until I finished high school. She was a court reporter before she married my father. But not every woman wants to stay home and care for a family. Many opt out to pursue their life's work."

"This is true, Steve, and they pursue their life's work for a good reason, since marriages go south too often, and they're left helpless, needing to enter the labor force unprepared and with small children to care for. Don't you see these challenges that women face when they have to choose between staying home full time, or going out to build financial independence, and all of it while they're married? They don't see the two goals as mutually exclusive. On the contrary, it gives them an added measure of security, reduces their dependance on their men—"

"Alright, I get it. I do. I'm just sick of this whole love thing. Do we even need to couple off? I'm tired of it. I'm kaput."

I embraced him, awkward as it was for both of us. "Look, Steve," I said, "this is simply my impression of Samentha. She's a lot like Abi in some ways, I suspect. Both these women will remain solo runners. You have to make up your mind fast whether you think Sam is the sort of woman you're looking for. And remember that, some days, *you'll* be the one cooking and putting Eleanor to bed while Sam works a night shift. And so on."

He pursed his lips, head tilted slightly, and sucked on a tooth. "You're talking to a defense attorney here! I hear what you're saying, and this is why I have to spend more time with you and less with my parents. Although I confess I *did* want to ask you. . . ."

A few moments went by before I asked, "What?"

"What makes you so sure that you know Samentha well enough to make these assumptions? What if she isn't even *interested* in getting remarried? Even after this evening, and the little bit of time you've spent with her. . .neither of us know her well enough to assume things, do we?"

"You're right. She's been my neighbor for what, maybe six hours? But my hunches come from my experience, you know? I don't think I'm that far off."

He nodded. "Alright, my friend, I think we should call it a day. I've got two court appearances downtown in the morning, and one is just an awfully messy case. . .this guy asks for seventy-five grand from our client for injuries suffered on the job, yet he cannot prove these injuries are related to his current employer or his previous one."

"What's your main argument?"

"One of them is that, sometimes, injuries take place years before symptoms show up. Some don't appear for ten years after the supposed injury."

The two of us carried on a while longer, until he realized he had misplaced his keys, which enabled us to focus less on conversation and more on turning in for the night. As I started stacking the dishes in the dishwasher, Steve played one more song on my piano. When the climax approached, I lay down onto the couch, closing my eyes just for a minute. I felt a migraine coming on.

CHAPTER FOUR

BURSERA FAGAROIDES

AND THEN, WITHOUT WARNING, I HAD TUMBLED backward into the past. The landline sat low on the stool next to my bed, ringing away as if it knew I was avoiding whoever was on the other end, toward the sound itself, but instead of getting up I let the ringing dissolve into my morning thoughts as I looked around the small, dark bedroom. It wasn't a place I felt a great connection with, a temporary rental I felt was much more comfortable admiring my space than something that meant much to me. Eventually I'd get set up elsewhere, perhaps out of town for a bit. But that wouldn't happen so soon. The room I was renting was close enough to Northridge State University that it barely took a few minutes for me to walk to campus. Although I'd stayed up the night before far past my limits—to be exact it was a quarter past two when I finally called it quits, during my preparation for the final exam. Electrical Engineering. Not exactly what I lay in bed dreaming about, but it was a helpful tool for me, nonetheless.

Looking over my shoulder now with eyes half open, I managed to make sense of the tiny screen on the alarm. Only 3:00 a.m. How could it be? The numbers blared in red on the clock, burning into my hangover.

And the phone began to ring again.

"Aw, heck!" I muttered, picking up the receiver, and in a faint voice said, "This is Joseph."

"Leo Turner here. You have three hours to get to LAX and board a special El-Al flight back home."

"Alright then, Leo. Let's hear it."

"Joseph, the Egyptians crossed the Suez Canal in the early hours of the morning, and at this point they're advancing quite quickly to the north. We've spotted about four brigades fully mobilized, with artillery and tanks. You will be picked up at Ben Gurion at 1300 Israeli time. You will then be brought to the base. Your orders are waiting for you. See you tomorrow, Joseph."

I didn't get another word in, and by 7:00 a.m. I was already in the air. I'd have about fourteen hours to prepare mentally for the mission. But I would think fondly of being in class instead.

I was mildly distracted most of the flight, wishing that I hadn't picked up the phone. But they would have reached me eventually. So I had to stay focused on the mental preparations. Digest the conversation with Turner. The captain's eyes were particularly swollen that evening, but even so he reminisced for a moment or so about flying combat missions with Joseph in the late Sixties, sitting in the back seat of the two-seater, a French-built bomber that was used to fly over the Suez Canal during the War of Attrition. That had been what followed the Six-Day War, what felt to be an endless, bewildering struggle between Israel and Egypt, ending in a cease-fire truce in late 1969.

Captain Turner was a navigator; I was the pilot. We carried out sorties over the canal in that period. The captain used maps and compasses and calculated the flight route to the targets. He was the eyes on my back and played a significant role in carrying out those bombing missions successfully.

Upon my arrival on the base, he greeted me, and I at once noted his higher rank. I was saluting the head of the squadron.

"When did you become a major?"

"Well, Joseph, some of us stayed behind while others left to pursue their dreams abroad. You got a taste of it. I hope that you got some good tail while you were still in one piece. But when did I become a major. Hm. Fuck. I can't say that it was a choice, more my duty. Who knows how long I've been in this role? I try not to think too much about time these days."

"Yeah, well, you sure interrupted my dream alright. I'd barely been asleep one hour when you woke me up on the phone."

"We need you to fly bombing missions tomorrow to halt the advancing Egyptian armies over in the Sinai. I'll introduce you to your navigator shortly, but now my driver will take you up to the living quarters to rest a bit. And after dinner, we'll debrief you back here at 2000. . . . It's good to see you, partner. I just wish it were under different circumstances, but this is the Middle East, and one never knows what tomorrow will bring."

"Agreed, Major Turner," I replied, and watched him disappear into a waiting Jeep. I was thirsty. I needed a shave, wished that I'd told that brunette back in California, the one with the fox tattooed on her ankle. . .I should have told her she was a looker, alright. As I sat up in my seat, I also thought about the very last time I had sat in a cockpit, almost two years before.

"He is of course, taking a hell of a chance, to include me in the four-bomber formation tomorrow. That son of a bitch," I said out loud to myself. Though, as head of the squadron, a major can make these decisions at any time whatsoever. Yes, it has been said that choosing the four pilots for the job was almost like an invitation into nothingness. Anything that went wrong could lead to his immediate resignation. No sentiments in the air force. And I may not have been up to the task, but it was happening. If I survived, I'd write to that brunette. Tell her she's cute. Ask her to wait for me. . .although that might be too sudden. So what does it matter if the major took the calculated risk? He knew me well enough.

But the pressure becomes exhausting in itself.

THE FLIGHT BEHIND ME NOW, I WAS LOOKING FORWARD to something warm to eat and catching up on a little more sleep. For about three hours, I'd been out like a light on the plane. There was something about flying that eased my worries. It was comforting, a similar feeling to when I would wake up in my bedroom--knowing that my time there was temporary, and that I would soon be where I was destined. The semester would come to an end, and I'd be able to lounge beneath a great cypress growing on the beach, the sun in my eyes as I faded in and out of slumber, three shots of gin under my belt.

But this was no time to fantasize, I realized as I recalled one last task before anything else—I had to phone my parents, who were at Brenner Hill, south of Tel Aviv.

"Hello?"

"Dad! It's me. Joseph! "

"My son, my son! The war broke out this morning, and Major Turner called us. He. . .he asked us how you could be reached. They needed you to fly."

"I'll be debriefed soon at the squadron," I told him. "And, well, I got here a few hours ago. I don't know when I'll get a chance to see you and Mom. I barely got a night's rest. Please send Mom my love."

"Be careful, son, and don't be a hero. You're the only one we've got." My father was always the one to admit to a great fear first, choking on the last words, whatever they were. During the Six-Day War, Papa had lost his best friend over the Suez Canal. The plane had received a direct hit by a ground-to-air Sam missile. Papa Joseph (he'd named his only son after himself) had managed to dodge the incident, but his very best friend hadn't been not so lucky. And he never forgot that image of the rolling aircraft, engulfed in red and yellow flames, on its way to the ground. He had been hoping to see the white parachute open, because a second chance was always in the cards, or so one would hope. But his father had waited and waited for that flare of white to fill the sky, waited for an hour, staring out into the abyss.

The body had never been recovered.

"WE WILL FLY IN A FOUR-FORMATION AT FIRST LIGHT TOMORROW," the major began in low voice. "We will fly at an altitude of 500 feet, to avoid detection. I will lead the formation. Our targets are the bridges over the Canal, those that enable the Egyptian armies to cross over onto to our side. Captain Joseph is my Number 2. We have 50 seconds to stay in the area, as we are well aware that the Russians supplied Sam missile batteries to the Egyptians. Our radars have complications detecting them in time, so avoiding them will be key. Focus now, men."

In missions of this nature, the aircraft ascends from a low altitude to a higher one in order to release its payload. The craft will dive again to exit the area.

"Joseph, Lieutenant Barak is your navigator. He's a veteran flyer, and he's familiar with the topography and the target. Pay attention, son. He'll get you to the target in a minimum amount of time. And to the rest of you tonight—remember the directives:You are not allowed to attack the target again in case you miss it with your first attempt, since the target area is infested with 5A2 and SA3 ground-to-air missiles, in addition to ground-to-air anti-aircraft artillery. Good luck. God knows you'll need it.

"Joseph, hang on a second. I know it's been about two years since you flew, since we last saw each other, but still—I have total confidence in you. I also feel some responsibility to your family. You return safely, or I will have a very hard time facing your mother and father. I made a promise to your mom that I would bring you back in one piece. Don't make a liar out of me, Captain."

"Roger that," I shot back. How was this even bearable? I had barely slept for five hours before reaching the squadron. Lieutenant Barak and I were driven to the hanger, where the bomber was waiting. I began to carry out some small talk with the ground crew. Although I didn't recognize any of those young faces, they knew my name, since they were expecting me. I circled the plane for preflight inspection and said I didn't notice anything unusual. Five-hundred-kilogram napalm bombs were secured under each wing, and there were nine 250-kilogram bombs in the belly of the bomber.

The time had come to defend. The ground crew moved some equipment out of the way. My navigator climbed into the back seat, followed by me. I settled into the cockpit with confidence. Being six feet tall wasn't an ideal height for a fighter jet pilot, but I was an exception. The cockpit itself was rather snug, small, and isolating. Yet the space could be bulky enough for a tall, relatively rotund pilot, unlike the cockpit on a commercial airline. My navigator was 5'10 and much more slender than me.

But all that was detail; we were at a crossroads. My navigator furrowed down the hatch doors, which were directly above us. We were at once given the signal to proceed and make our exit. In very little time, we were airborne.

It was an early morning in October, the clouds low, sedentary, collapsing into the sky. We tried to stay beneath them, to prevent early detection. Three other planes came up beside us, and were on our way.

AT 6:00 A.M., I GOT OUT OF BED; as one who rises on the earlier side, I was feeling a bit lighter than usual, though I still could taste the remnants of my migraine in the back of my throat, the dry mouth, and too many trips to the lavatory throughout the night. A symposium of doubt awaited me, imposing their weight on me as such entities tends to do.

Sam and Nora were the first things on my mind each and every morning, as if they were a song I had memorized without consent. I hadn't seen them in days. Perhaps I had been a little busier than usual the past week, since, now that Abi had returned, she was my priority.

But something was missing even so. I stumbled into the kitchen for some hot tea and a little cereal—but no milk this time. I went into the den to catch up on recent headlines, but on my computer, rather than the steady pile of newspapers that sat patiently awaiting my arrival, at the corner of the dining room table. I hadn't dreamt about '73 in so long, you can say that the unexpected reminder was a bit troublesome for me.

I'm not sure what was happening, but I was completely stuck in the odd feeling all morning, so much that I read seven different articles, although I didn't finish one of them all the way though. Perhaps I should try and get some more sleep? One more rapid eye movement, just another forty-five minutes? Then I'll get a shower. More tea too—no coffee today felt like the right sort of thing.

TWO HOURS LATER, AT ALMOST 8:00 A.M., THE DOORBELL RANG. Was I expecting anyone? I asked myself. It had been six weeks since my new neighbors moved in. I was no longer a stranger to young Elie. Although it had been a few days since I'd seen them around, I was trying not to think about it too much. That may have been the only helpful aspect of being in the war, the ability to turn oneself off. They teach it to you in AA as well, I've heard, to simply make no big deal out of anything. But how long can people go about numbing themselves?

But the door! I must not get distracted now. I slipped into my gray sweatshirt and a pair of old jeans. Should I lose the house slippers? They're so warm, and with December's arrival. . .honestly, I even dreaded leaving the apartment without my slippers. As I make my way to the door, my goodness, my hair is a mess. Let me comb it back. And I didn't get that shower. But then I heard her voice, and suddenly nothing else mattered.

"Joseph! Oh, Joseph, are you home?" came the child's voice from behind the door. Maybe I'm lonelier than I can admit. Do I wish that Abi and I'd had a child? I could never confess these things to her, and I'm already past my prime. To have a child now would be. . .would be, well, it would be kinda grand.

The child is patiently standing outside my door with her back pack on, holding her pink lunch box at her side. Her eyes are somewhat hidden by her little baseball cap, this time a green one with the brim lined in yellow. There's a slight breeze, one that I've been awaiting. The changing of the seasons, again, is a feeling that is unlike any other. When one hears fire engines and street hounds singing along to the same obnoxious melody, often interrupted by the passing of a dozen single mothers with their strollers, some good friends and others just acquaintances.

"Morning, Elie. Heading out to school, then, are you, and you came to wish me good morning first?"

"Yes and no," she said, kicking at the door frame and bending down to pick up one of those Japanese beetles that will often keel over at twilight.

"What do you mean, yes and no? Do you need a ride to school today?"

"Well, I'm not ready to *go* to school until Mom is feeling better. It's something she said with her head. If Daddy were here, he would do something about it. But I talked to him this morning, when I was brushing my hair. I asked him—well, first I asked God if she would bring Daddy back, but she said it just wasn't possible. So I asked her to ask him if he could help Mommy feel better. But then—" Nora leaned in closer, whispering, "Well, then Daddy told me Mommy had to find someone else to help her. But that he was close by."

"Oh, my goodness, Elie! Can you tell me what's wrong with your mom? Did she hit her head?"

"No, no! She called it something that starts with an 'M.' She told me that she needs medicine. Do you have any medicine?"

"Tell her, my dear, that I'll be right over. Alright, sweetie?"

I went into the kitchen to grab a few things for them, some fruit and something to drink. Perhaps it was a hangover. I went into my bedroom to bring along my phone, in case theirs wasn't working—who knows? I've got to be prepared for the worst. And although I was worried, something came over me, and it's strange for me to admit to this, but with Sam and Elie around, I don't miss Abi as much.

"Sam? Hello there. . .anyone home? I hear you need a Dr. Joseph on the premises?" I added playfully as I stumbled through the front door with my bag of nectarines and some alkaline water, just in case.

But no one answered right away. Something must be terribly wrong, I thought. I've never seen so many dishes on their kitchen counter. And amid the decor, there was more of a mess, the usual adornments that would be expected—towels in a pile by the television, mail in stacks on the couch. But alongside all of this was my favorite part of their home, which consisted of Samentha's most adored plant specimens, the Bursera fagaroides (in bright orange pots, mind you) that grew boldly beneath the bay windows in the kitchen. Somehow, Sam was able to grow an abundance of succulents indoors, which is often an impossible feat to accomplish.

"Who's there?" asked a familiar voice. And there she lay, dear Samentha, half atop the sofa in the living room. She wore a red house robe, and her hair was a bit disheveled. I could see her dinner from the night before on the dining room table, and her eyes were red as they scrolled back and forth through the mess surrounding the two of us.

"Well, Joseph, I guess you caught me at my worst. That's what a bustling friendship is all about, don't you think? Hand me that glass of water, will you?"

"Of course. Here you go. What happened to you, if you don't mind my asking?"

"I got behind at work, so I decided to take a leave of absence, but I took some documents home—just paperwork that I needed to take care of that I'd been putting off. It's this *migraine* I can't get rid of. Every single month, Jo, like a Swiss clock."

I didn't tell her that I had been suffering a migraine the night before, but I offered to pick up her prescription at the pharmacy next door. It was just one building over, on Wilshire. The pharmacist and I had known each other for years by then.

"Can I come with you?" Nora pleaded. "Mom, I want to go with Jo to the store, I really need some new, umm. . . ."

"Some new what? What could you possibly need more of, my little sparkplug?" Samentha scooped Nora into her arms and began blowing bubbles on her cheeks; the two squealed and eventually pulled me into the mix, where I suddenly had the girl with the pink glasses on top of my shoulders, and we were chasing Mama around the apartment. . .at a respectable pace that is, as Sam was weak but not so terribly out of shape that she couldn't handle the situation.

Eventually everything calmed down a bit, and I set Eleanor down onto the couch next to her mother.

"You should stay with your mom, Elie. It'll just be for a few minutes that I'll be at the pharmacy, to pick up that medicine. And then, we'll send you off to school, and of course I'll take the next shift here while you go and learn to your heart's desire with all your friends!"

"You're a lifesaver, Joseph. Where have you been all these years? God, these migraines nearly kill me. If you only knew, which I hope you never will, what these spells do to me."

"Well, Samentha, I can't argue that I have no idea what you're talking about."

"What's that?" she asked with her mouth wide open.

"I have this, this awful condition myself. The rainbow auras, the sensitivity to light—"

"The nausea, food cravings, and constipation?" she continued, and she was right.

"Oh, and I am much too old for constipation. But see, my father had them too, the migraines. . .it's purely genetic for me."

"As far as I remember, my mother never had a headache, not even when she'd go through her monthly spell. Of course menopause changed all that. But I have had such strange luck throughout my life, and this dreaded curse started when I was about twelve. It was right at that time when I started to notice other girls were shaving their legs at school. I dread that day for Nora sometimes."

"Yes, I can only imagine all the delicate stresses of being a girl at that age. I'm sorry, Sam. But don't you worry, I'll head off to the pharmacy. We'll catch up more later, alright?"

"But Joseph?" Sam suddenly pleaded, in a different sort of tone now. She sat up and closed her eyes for a second.

I leaned over and pulled her hair back behind her ears, straightened her blanket out so that it covered her shoulders as well as her toes. "Yeah Sam, what is it?"

"Stay just a little longer today, if you have the chance," she asked, with her blonde whisps of hair entangled within the straps of her bra, as the little one lay down on the floor, counting out loud all of the various shades of blue and pink, these subtle reflections from the sun pouring through the bay windows. For a moment I could hear someone coming up the stairwell and disappearing off into the echo of Nora's voice counting each and every sunbeam on the ceiling. It was noon already, and I had promised Abigail I would meet her later at the Melting Pot.

It's one of those organic restaurants, a spot we often frequent and not too far away— Melrose and Doheny. Abi is a sucker for the organic chef salads, especially with the house dressing. She was never very picky with other delicacies, and I liked that about her. She knew what she wanted, and it would at times allow for me to think more about things I preferred on this road of life. But once in a while I felt she was being extra flexible with certain decisions just to spite me. So I arrived with the moon a crescent splendor. I felt heavy inside, as if I was arriving at a place that I hadn't been to in years.

I took a moment to look at myself in the rear-view mirror, at my eyes, and for a second I did feel my age. I wondered when death would come for me, and if I would be at home, with Abigail, or at the market. Would I take my last breath next to Nora? She could sing me a melody she learned in school, hold my hand, and tell me that everything was going to be alright. I even got this vision of teaching her to drive, when she reached those dreaded teenage years.

Enough fantasizing, Joseph. You're getting carried away. At times, though, I wondered if this was actually all a dream? I turned off the ignition and at the entrance to the joint: families storming through the front door, a man on a ladder adjusting the main lights above the scaffold. I watched a couple of twenty-year-olds barrel straight through a crowd of elderly women standing at the front, docile ladies awaiting their ride, or perhaps just about to go inside. So I climbed out of my head, got out of the car, and handed my keys to the attendant, as I tend to do.

"If you don't mind, please put her in a safe place while I'm gone." I handed the young man five dollars and made my way in.

Abigail, in all of her glory, was already seated and holding a glass of white wine. She was my Abi, and I shouldn't complain. But the truth is that there are differences between us. Although we fell for each other all those years back, some things just didn't match up. At our core, we wanted different things in life. I'd love for her to move in, but she prefers her space.

"Jack! Over here, love! Shall I order us the usual?"

"Yes! Please do!" I shouted back. The restaurant opened only a few months ago, although it was decorated as if it had been there for decades. Vibrant plants hung from the ceiling, and yellow lights adorned the walls surrounding us. Paintings of female dancers with strong legs, wide hips, and small breasts in flowery red dresses—echoes of Al Green and, once in a while, a classic disco song. Our kind of joint.

I ordered a beer on tap and felt like a veggie burger, to be honest with you. Perhaps a small cup of soup. The combination was something I looked forward to; I believe they call it the Peasant Lunch.

"Tell me, doll," she asked after the food came, "what were you doing this morning besides nursing your migraine? And how are you feeling? Oh, can I have the pepper? Thank you, honey."

"Oddly enough, I got wrapped up helping another migraine patient."

"Oh? One of your neighbors?"

"It's the new tenants across from me, you know, the daughter, Eleanor?"

"And Samentha, the mother, yes. They're a little needy, are they? So soon upon their arrival?"

"Well, yeah. Sam was in pretty bad shape. I went ahead and ran an errand for her, then saw Nora off to school."

"I see you've really established yourself while I've been gone!"

"It's true. When you're out of town, I tend to get quite caught up in my own life. But I barely see my neighbors, much less attend to them asking for help. I don't want to be that guy everyone comes to. Then I'll never have to—"

"Play a new song on your piano? I do miss those nights. Let's make tonight one of those special events, when I come back with you after lunch, and we snuggle on the couch to a good movie. Take a nap, wake up, and order out. Instead of wine, we'll bake something sweet—carrot cake you love. You still love carrot cake, don't you?"

"Oh, Abi. That sounds delightful."

"Will you play me a few songs as well? Just two or three?"

"Of course I will," I said, feeling a blush coming on. At times I wonder if I should just ask her to move in. We're getting older, and there's no way to deny what's to come. Why waste time? Although having our own homes outside of the relationship, I do find myself rather used to that whole arrangement. I get some of my best sleep, alone, in my bed.

"So how's your neighbor coming along in the big city, then? It's been a couple of months now since they showed up, right?"

"Almost, just about. But to tell you the truth, Abi, it feels like I've known them for much longer ."

"How so? Like old friends?"

"Can't exactly explain it." I paused and looked at the view outside the restaurant, searching for words; yet for the first time she and I had been together, I couldn't find anything to say beyond a sigh and a forced smile.

"At the risk of sounding juvenile," she said, "I can't help but wonder if you're developing some sort of—of an attachment to them. Are you feeling alright? Just tell me. I'm here to listen. You know me." Abigail was always so flexible. She could go from romantic to tomboy in seconds. And rarely did she get jealous.

But my obsession with Sam and Nora had been growing, and I may have been too obvious in revealing it to those around me. "The answer is yes. I'm just in a whirlwind. I can't get either of them out of my mind. It just feels so natural, this connection."

"I suspected as much. Where do I fit in the new picture, Jack? Should I be alarmed, or am I totally off target here?"

"This is all new to me. I do so enjoy interacting with them, and especially with the little one. She's like the daughter and grandchild I never had. And I did want to come to you with this as it was happening. I just didn't want it to, well, didn't want you to worry. About us. Even though we have our magic, you have to admit, it's a complicated relationship in certain ways. The distance between us."

"I know, honey. It's, yeah. . .we've somehow drifted apart—if we really look at it realistically. I feel responsible for your happiness. Your safety."

"As do I, Abi."

"I guess if we were truly committed, we'd just move in together, finally. After all this time. What are we so frightened of? I don't know."

"I don't know either by now."

"So these two girls, they're important to you? You feel an affinity. . . ? "

"Our friendship is something that I need in my life. It's as if something inside of me has been awakened." Perhaps that was too much. No one's partner wants to hear that they're not the great sanctuary in the relationship. But If I'm not honest now, how can I sleep at night?

So I continued, "Abi, I love you. Yet somehow, with these two people new to my life, it was as if I'd awakened from a long-overdue slumber. I'm turning sixty-one in January, and I feel that some void in my life is being filled up. I'm purposefully, at this point—call me crazy if you will, but I am making room for more feelings to enter, to occupy my mind. Even so, I feel this responsibility looking after two vulnerable women, who just landed in this awful city."

"I'm listening. I hear you, Joseph."

"Of course, I have my promise to you—with what we have built together. I'm sorry, Abi, it's just that these new tenants have added meaning to my daily routine that truly excites me. The bottom line is that I'm happier and more alive now. And I'm hoping that will only enhance *our* relationship, enriching it in many ways that were not so available before."

But what I really wanted to say was that I had secretly hoped I'd one day run off to Oregon with Sam and Nora, to start a new life. And that I would meet another lover, eventually, or not. I didn't want to lose Abi. But I couldn't imagine going much further down the road of life, feeling a deeper connection to these two women, without being able to continue to grow closer together.

"This is certainly the first time I've noticed your true gift," she said, "how you interact with children. I never imagined it was in you to have so much patience like that. I certainly don't get carried away with a child the way you do. Maybe you're right—we *are* very different. And that's not something I was ready to look at or admit to."

"I'm surprised as well. It's one of those unexpected things life throws at you, I suppose." I'd better stop while I'm ahead, I was thinking. There was nothing for Abi to really be jealous of, but to be honest with myself, that wasn't exactly true. With Sam, I just purely enjoyed our conversations in a way that I had yet to put words to. There hadn't been a thing we couldn't talk about. At times, hours would pass, and we simply never ran out of things to enjoy together.

You'd think, as with most friendships, that eventually two people tire of one another. But with Samentha and me, and young Eleanor, there was not one dull moment. You could argue that it's usually how things feel when you first get to know someone. But I hadn't had this feeling ever before. I couldn't shake either the sense that it was destiny in some shape or form. Now, I have no room in my life for the absurdity of the esoteric arts, but sometimes there are other forces at play in situations like the one I was in. And one cannot simply ignore something so magnificent.

"Well, tell me," Abi asked, "how's Steve doing these days? I haven't seen him in a while."

"He seems fine. He stopped by yesterday, and his visits are, actually, more frequent now. Last week he took Samentha out to dinner and a movie while I was babysitting the little one, reading to her, we even played a game of chess! She's that bright. I tell you, it blows my mind. Can you picture me doing all that? And right before I put her down to bed, she asks me thousands of questions."

"Such as?"

"She asked me about how lightbulbs are made, why the sun gets so hot, if she wanted to grow up to be a chairmaker if that would be okay for a girl to do, and so many other things. Why there are cement ladies out on the balcony, and if those ladies were bad and that's why they were turned into cement! I mean, it's just incredible the things she thinks of."

"Eleanor will get quite attached to you if she hasn't already. I may not know much about the tendencies of children, but I do know that they get attached. Even if you only saw her once every year, she would remember you. It's something about the elasticity of their brains."

"I don't recall being that excited about learning when I was younger."

"Ah, but you grew up in a different time, a different world. Israel, honey, is not Los Angeles."

"Of course—no, that's true. But she is just so mature for her age. She thinks of things I'd never even questioned. She asked me, that night, what I would do if, one morning, I awoke and the sky was lemon yellow, and the grass was purple! And I didn't know how to respond, but the vision of this other world through her eyes was just so lovely."

"I may have been stubborn. Having separate homes, living our lives in ways that most couples didn't—I thought it was actually quite sexy."

"Yeah, I did, too. For a while there, Abi. I did."

"And I should have been more aware, in certain ways, of our age difference. Perhaps I was naive. I don't know why I never wanted to have a child. I guess you could say I didn't trust that I had it in me."

"I'm glad we can talk about this. Can I tell you something else that young girl asked me?"

"Might as well put it all out on the table!" Abigail poured us both another glass of wine and took a few gulps, gasping for air afterwords and staring at me with those wild eyes.

"As she was falling asleep and her dialogue became a bit more subdued, she—this little one—asked me if I loved her mom. She asked me if I would marry her, so that she wouldn't miss her dad so much. Of course I said no, since I'm not interested in Sam in that way, plus she's dating Steve now, and the two of them are something together. There's a lot of chemistry."

"Steve is going for it huh? Wow. So he booted what's her face then, did he? Kathy is out of the picture. . .I thought they were serious."

"Some drawn-out complication with her schooling. Kathy is leaving the state to pursue her studies in Colorado. I can't say that I didn't see it coming."

"Yeah, they were kind of a drag together."

"That they were. I always thought Steve could do better."

"And you think he's ready to jump into a new relationship so quickly? A situation involving very different responsibilities. . .a young girl is a handful."

"I've had a few conversations with him on the subject. I've always felt that Steve was self-aware, intelligent, perceptive, a little old-fashioned for his generation, but I talked him through it."

"So how exactly did you tell this little girl, by the way, that you weren't interested in marrying her mother? This I gotta hear." Abi sat back in her chair, folded her arms tightly across her chest, and smiled that somewhat demanding smile that always made me nervous—but nervous in the sense that I wanted to tell her what I imagined she wanted to hear. And yet for some reason, this time around, I said what I had to say regardless of her expectations.

"Eleanor told me, she said that. . .well, when other dads come to pick up her classmates from school, that she's a bit jealous, feeling very envious of that, which is missing from her life. It's been only, I think, three years since she lost her father. His memory, however minuscule, is still alive in her heart."

And that was the last thing I said to Abi, aside from asking the waiter for the check. We made our way out to the front of the restaurant and stood there for a few minutes in silence.

The temperature was cooling off the way that it tends to in L.A. in late December. Finally that embrace of winter was to come to us inhabitants of the wretched city. In many respects, I was waiting for that time of the year.

But was this home until the end of time? Abi never cared much for the chillier climate. I put my arms around her while the attendant brought the car. Looking up at the sky together, we sighed at the way the clouds formed their silly patterns, perhaps even contemplating what would come next in our relationship. Would we take this opportunity to ask more questions about "us," or would things instead continue the way they were—with infrequent visits, stories shared over a telephone call from Madrid, memories never created, dialogues in a busy diner, all of the things that triggered the initial spark between us. It was almost as if we had never left the courting stage, never taking it a step further. Our circle of friends did admire us for being so unconventional, and that was often an exciting feature to brag about: living like a bachelor but having someone to share moments of intimacy with, minus the ball-and-chain dilemma. But were we ever really "together"?

I put my jacket around Abigail's lovely shoulders and gently helped her into her car, a cozy red Jaguar she'd bought years before, not exactly something she had planned—she'd won a lawsuit, truth be told, and when a decent chunk of money comes in one must invest. We kissed goodbye for just a second and held each other a little longer than usual, with the plan to "meet up again soon, love. For lunch the next afternoon."

ON MY WAY HOME I DECIDED TO DRIVE by Eleanor's school. There was a chance that she would be playing on the grounds, and after such a rather depressing lunch with Abigail, I needed a moment to recalibrate. A simple glance from afar at Nora's smile was all I needed.

"Strange, isn't it?" I said out loud to myself. How odd that a little girl had entered my heart so suddenly. And I knew that her mother needed me, in the way that any person so vulnerable yet independent is, no matter how stable and structured she might be. We all need someone in our lives, to allow for the days to drift by with more luster and meaning.

At times I think I'm overthinking all of this. That one morning I could awake to the sound of a moving truck below the balcony at the apartment, coming to take away the two people who'd rushed into my life as if my dreams had been answered. As if someone, up there, actually cared.

My thoughts got lost amid an extended honking of a car horn so loud and piercing that I almost imagined I was in bed, falling asleep to an action film on the television. But I was awake, and the light was green. How long had I been parked there?

I drove West on Melrose, toward the Ocean. The sun was blinding me; it was 1:30. And descending above Santa Monica Boulevard, I made my way slowly to the Pacific. Right on Camden Street, I approached the fenced-in schoolyard. I sat there in my car at the nearby red light, hoping to spot the girl with the pink glasses. Many children were running around, teasing one another, a few playing a game of kickball, while others were lying on the cement, most likely discussing things like colored pencils, applesauce stains on their sweaters, maybe even the color of the marigolds off at the edge of the schoolyard, or some new chocolate-malted snack that one of their fathers had secretly slipped into their sack lunch that day.

But Eleanor, to my surprise, was nowhere to be seen. I needn't worry, though, I told myself. Just go home.

Besides, Steve was stopping by that evening for a drink, and I needed to tell him I wasn't sure if I wanted him to see more of Samentha so soon.

"SO, STEVE, TELL ME. . . ."

"Tell ya' what, pops? What's on your mind tonight?" He was enthusiastic, I could tell. And I guess you could say there was a `lot` on my mind.

"I had very different sort of lunch today, with Abi. Maybe you can offer some advice on the subject."

"She's leaving you?"

"No, not exactly."

"You had a nice time, yeah? Made out a little, for old times sake?"

"No, no, it wasn't like that at all. It was a bit more complicated. But nothing I'm alarmed about."

"She's pregnant!"

"Steve! Come on, I, uh. . .pregnant, no. Oh, dear. . . ."

"You're a bundle of nerves tonight. What's going on? Talk to me. Tell Steve all your woes."

"I wanted to know your impression of Samentha." Perhaps that wasn't how I should have started.

"I do *like* her. I do, Joseph. Very much so, in fact." He cleared his throat, got up, and paced around me for a minute in silence. "We've been having quite a time together," he went on. "She just brings the best out in me. Don't you remember us together at your place that one morning? I was completely smitten just seeing her so briefly."

"You had me a bit worried, of course," I said. "You wanted to take her to bed right away."

"Now, don't you paint me that way. I have the best intentions for her."

"That's all I needed to know. She's vulnerable right now."

". . .You're taking this a little seriously, aren't you?" He sat up straight across from me, licking his lips and looking at his shoes, raising his legs up in the air for a second, muttering something about where he'd bought the shoes, and about how he was sick of drinking the same kind of lager during our visits. He then looked up at me and started to laugh to himself. "Look, Joseph, I'm no mind reader. What's going on here? Did Sam mention me to you at all?"

"Yes, she brought you up."

"And what's my report card so far?"

"You, my friend, have gotten a solid B+."

"Oh, no! Wait a second here—you're fully aware that I'm not a B student. I passed the bar, first sitting! I made junior partner in five years, which never happens. Plus I'm winning most of my cases, the majority of them! And I'm not skirting across any dishonest grounds."

"I hear you, but Samentha isn't that easy to win over. She's more complicated than any of your most difficult cases. But she did say that you're moving a bit too fast." Feeling on edge, I looked at him straight in the eye and awaited his response.

"She *said* that to you? That I was moving too fast?"

"Indeed."

"And your response was. . . ?"

"I told her that you may feel a bit needy right now, with your recent rejection from Kathy. How that can be a motivating factor to your fascination with her, but that overall you have a good heart."

"Oy, a good heart. But desperate, right? I'm just another guy she's gonna eventually dismiss--and lucky me, you'll be there to rub it all in my face. All the while, I'm in court, fighting for these dipshits and, Oh God, those uptight opposing attorneys I could give a rat's ass about. . . . Joseph, I deal with rejection each and every day. Often my argument is rejected by the opposing attorney until the case is settled. There was this nurse who filed for compensation, complaining that her back was going out due to lifting bedridden patients for the past twenty-five years. And she failed to mention that she's only been working for two years at this current hospital, so I demanded that she instead sue the *previous* hospitals she had been employed by, to reduce the liability of my client—"

"Steve, just stop there. That's enough. We're talking about Samentha. Will you calm down? Get it together. I'm too goddamn old for this."

"You don't know *my life*. You don't know what I go through when I'm not at your beck and call." He ran over to my piano and began to play a frantic tune. I ignored him for a minute, then walked over and put my hands on his shoulders. He stopped playing and began to laugh. And when this guy starts to chuckle, I tell you it's quite contagious.

"I'm really embarrassed right now. You're such a pal—in your own stubborn way." He turned around and grabbed me around my torso, squeezing me a little too tightly. But I can't argue that I didn't need that moment just then.

"I'm sorry," I said. "I *am* quite protective of her."

"It's in your nature. And I've got this temper that's somehow erupted over the years. I really need to work on this, especially if I'm going to be in Nora's life."

So maybe he'd realized what was actually happening, that a young girl was part of it, and that I had every right to defend them, to ask questions. . .maybe even that I was a better father than my own dad ever was, in a spiritual manner.

I decided to keep going with the dialogue. Granted it was already reaching a boiling point. "That's what Abigail and I got into today. I told her more in detail on little Eleanor, and of course Samentha. Steve, I love Abi. And as I reluctantly admitted to her, this little girl and this one woman, they've arrived at a time when I really needed someone. At a time when I knew that my loneliness was going to get the better of me. I told Abi that it was as if I had woken up from a long-overdue slumber Sam and Nora came into my life."

He sat back down across from me on the couch. "They *are* quite special, aren't they?"

"Yes. They are. I feel this closeness to them both."

"You should have had kids, Joseph. It's all coming back to haunt you."

"You think I'm not aware of that? I am. I'm in it."

"To answer your question, and I owe it to you right now, it's true. Sam and I, we have only been holding hands, nothing more than that. I've pushed to move beyond that and make progress."

"Progress for whom, though? For Eleanor? She's at the top of that list."

"I know, but I can't think about the kid every fucking second. I want progress for Sam and me. She's a real woman, not just a mother. But she doesn't seem ready, and I may be on the rebound, as you've made quite clear to both Sam and me. So I'm resolved to be patient."

"I'm listening."

"Samentha, she—um, she keeps filling me in on her past. Her life growing up just a few miles away from where I was raised. Catching caterpillars at dawn, before class. I used to carry them in my pocket, then release them near the forest by the campus. Most of them would get completely squashed in my jeans on my way to where I'd set them free. Samentha told me that she'd had a whole terrarium of caterpillars at her flat, when she lived off campus. And later on down the line, when she and John were together there, I have to say I got jealous. She was very much in love. I can't exactly say I've ever felt that deeply for a gal. Well, not until I met her. Maybe it's all this adoration you've been sharing with me that's got me mixed up. But I do care for her. And it happened fast. I keep saying to myself that I'll take it at a slower pace, but I just can't help it."

"I still don't like that conversation we had that one day about you wanting her to be a stay-at-home mom. Remnants of that just don't sit right with me," I said, but I knew that it was no time to be bringing up past arguments. Could it be that all this mentoring of him tiring me? He rambled on, but I was soon barely paying attention. I'd had my doubts about him getting too close to her at the start. What had I gotten myself into?

". . .Are you even *listening* to me? *Hello?"* Steve could be such a misfit at times. It's a wonder we'd even lasted that long as friends. But my role as his father figure was to find the stillness and patience to listen and come up with solutions.

Yet once in a while I found the process to be absolutely exhausting. I found myself dreaming of being out on a boat somewhere away from the city, watching the pier get smaller and smaller as we drifted out to sea. Sam and Nora are there (how could they not be?), but I wasn't going to be barked at much more that night, with this man by my side who might as well just head home, for Chrissake.

"The thing is, I'm genuinely interested in her. Sam is just one of those girls that you can actually enjoy talking to. But this whole thing with the unfinished business and the sperm donor she never met, you know, her supposed father? How much should I invest in that? But at my age, would it make a difference? To know who this man might be is not going to be easy for Samentha, I imagine."

"She was telling me how she remembered asking her mother questions about him. Why was it that all her friends had their dads come to school to pick them up, and why it was that her grandmother was the one who took her home instead when school let out. Why she didn't have that nuclear family to respond to her each and every need. And now that she sees her *own* daughter without a father. . .well, I can see how she's gotten attached to you, Joseph. And you to her. I'm no dummy. I may be impatient and stubborn. But I'm aware of these things."

"My God," I said as I turned to the kitchen to make some coffee for us. It was going to be a long night, so we might as well be in a better head space. What do you tell a small child about the person with whom her own mother barely spent a month and then just disappeared, as if he'd never existed in the first place?

"So she told me that her grandmother wouldn't let her mom abort. In the 1970s, it was still an issue. Women flew to Japan or down to Mexico to have abortions. So she ended up being raised by her grandparents, and during this time her mother was working at a hospital. It all just sounds so rough. Maybe I shouldn't get mixed up in this whole legacy of sorts."

"What else do you know about the sperm donor?"

"Apparently, her mother didn't know much about this young man, but enough to fall for him over the course of a few days. And if you've heard these tales about the mother, I'll tell you --she was a tough cookie, and a babe. A total magnet. Oh, what was it Sam said? That her mother wasn't even sure if it was a local guy, since she never saw him again. Never heard from him down the line. She found out she was pregnant and just didn't think to try and contact this guy, assuming that he returned to his country, or wherever he may have been from, shortly after their encounter."

"Not even after she had the child, the mother didn't care to figure it out? The father of her first child?"

"From what I gathered, Sam asked her for decades why it was that she'd kept it a secret from him. And I guess she replied that she didn't think he would want to know, that he wouldn't believe her anyway and she didn't want to complicate the situation. Something along those lines."

"Say, Steve, did you mean it when you said you'd give Eleanor piano lessons?" Of course I hoped he'd back out, so that I could be the one to teach her the ways of the keys.

"Yeah—well, I'd like that very much, to teach that girl the piano. Especially now, knowing that Sam is closer to you, emotionally, than she is with me. It's asinine. I dunno, Joseph. I just want things to go back to how they were. You, me, and Abi out on the town. No real worries. Sure I'd take Kathy back. She was nice, you know? I may not have been in love with her, but there's this thing that—and stop me if this sounds like I'm being a little bitch—"

"It's too late for that—"

"Listen! Alright, I'm just going to throw this out there. What if we couple off with people who we feel 'safe' with but not completely enthralled by?"

"You mean we'd rather just be with some lady who's cute, smart, but not terribly interesting, the attainable lover who doesn't really ruffle anyone's feathers. Doesn't turn you on much, but they're there. So you might as well take them in. Although I felt that Abi was quite unattainable—she was, and still is, a fox. But we made out quite nicely."

"I was thinking, Joseph, knowing that one day Kathy would grow old and I'd see her off to her own death. It sounds awful, but when I think about the end of time and wonder who might be there by my side, I ask myself if it could be someone like Sam. Perhaps that scares me, but I want it. It's more of risk to be with someone you actually care about. Whereas if you're just with someone who's nice and stable, someone to come home to, it's not as frightening." He babbled on, and I handed him his cup of coffee. He breathed in the aroma and set it down onto the dining room table.

"Love is no easy stride, Steve. Real love appears to be so much more of a risk."

"Yeah, well, I think that Sam knows about you and Abigail, doesn't she? Just a little? They haven't yet met, but she knows of her."

"She does."

"Are you sure that she's not just stringing me along, while really she's trying to get the two of you to break up?"

"No, Steve. That's not the case."

"Then how do you explain her feeling so much more comfortable around you than she does around me?" He was going back and forth between arguing with me and having a decent discussion.

It was a red flag to not be messed with, but I didn't know for sure if it was truly my role to tell him what to do. Still, I had more to say. "I honestly have no clue, but competition from me you just don't have. I love Abi, and that's that."

"But aren't you attracted to younger women? After all, it's just our bodies that progress, we're still just fourteen-year-old kids looking for someone to soothe our teenage dreams. Correct me if I'm wrong, but don't younger women keep you feeling spry and childlike, make you feel that you can keep your old age at bay, as they say, for just a while longer. Just one more pathetic breath from your aging old lungs—"

"Oh, Steve, maybe we should call it a night already!"

"No, you're going to tell me right now—are you attracted to Samentha? Do you have intentions to take this friendship further? I'm not leaving until you give me an answer."

"She is attractive, she's alluring, of course, but not to *me*, Steve. And please, don't ask me why. It's your turn to commit and get on with your life. You're not getting younger, but don't lead her on with false hopes. Because if you do, I'll come to you right then and there and shout out, 'Objection, Your Honor!"

"Goddamn! why are you being so protective of someone you barely know, Joseph?"

"I'm silly, I suppose. I can't even explain my behavior to myself, much less to you. I tried with Abigail. Now she's on my case. I want you to take Samentha out tomorrow. I think it's her night off, and I'll be babysitting the little one."

"Hey, I don't take orders from you in the case of love, Joseph. If you love her, tell me now. If you don't, well then, I'll need some convincing. Either way, I'm pursuing this woman. And if she doesn't want me, I assume she'll tell me herself."

CHAPTER FIVE

ONLY A SHADOW

IF YOU'D ASKED ME A FEW MONTHS BACK whether I was prepared for what this year would bring, I'd have told you without hesitation that I was. I have been ready for this my entire life. But would I have remotely believed what was about to take place, no. I don't think I would have believed you, even if you provided me with proof, since I never did put much faith in dreams. I had always imagined miraculous happenings belonging to others.

That being said, I may have taken on a bit too much with my current situation. And Abi doesn't have time to waste on my inner dramas come to fruition—although I didn't come to terms with this whole thing until the very end of my story, and we're not there just yet. If I'm to be honest with you, you've stuck around this far, so perhaps you have some interest in what I have to tell you. Or maybe you're just lonely. Aren't we all?

Steve took Samentha out that night, the day after he and I had our big argument. The two went to the theatre for some hair-raising double feature starring Hedy Lamarr, but they left before the credits of the first film ran.

Steve was eager for conversation, since he had been feeling an uneasiness with Sam during the film. He'd made two attempts to hold her hand, and both times she hadn't let him.

They had found an empty aisle toward the middle of the theater and sat down together. Sam was exceptionally low in spirits, and any conversation she'd engage in was mostly surface stuff: how frustrating work had been, how she'd worn the wrong shoes on her morning jog, nothing that leant any meaning toward her interest in Steve.

Yet the extraordinary thing about Steve was that he was always able to cheer someone up, right out of their slump, all with very little effort on his end. But despite this talent, his charm wasn't the slightest bit effective that night. He handed her the soda she asked for, a diet Cherry Coke, and some thin mints. He took her hand into his and kissed her wrist. She pulled away.

Well, if she was going to do hard to get, he could play that game, too. He got up from his seat and started to slow dance with himself. The audience around them booed and shrieked —and he felt excited to rouse the crowd, although she tried to pretend his antics weren't the slightest bit adorable to her. "Steve, will you sit down, for Chrissake." She pulled him to his seat, and down he came, playful as a sprite, grabbing a few handfuls of popcorn and tossing them into the folks behind them.

And then she smiled, for the first time the entire night. Our heroine in crisis knew that Steve could be good for her, but she didn't want to give in right away. It'd been a while since she'd kissed anyone. He had a nice voice, and he was confident, successful, and never had bad breath. She approved of these amiable details.

But if she was to get a kiss, she'd decided that one thing had to happen first. She would have to meet his mother, to see how he treated her. . .the ultimate test. That's what would allow for her to open up and trust him a bit more than she'd allowed herself to thus far.

"Steve, look. . .I'm really sorry. It's just that I'm on edge tonight, and romance right now just makes me feel uneasy." But Sam knew that he must be suspicious: All this time together, and she wouldn't even hold his hand in a movie theater. Who was she trying to fool?

"I apologize, sweetheart. It's not in my nature to pressure you in that way. I just thought you looked so damn lovely in this light. Ya know? So let's enjoy the film, yeah?"

And those were the last words they exchanged for the rest of the film. He felt, not just confused, but in fact insulted. After three months of getting to know one another, not even a kiss or a hand to hold at the theatre? Was it turning into any type of a relationship, or had the moment already passed? He needn't bother bringing these things up, though, not now.

But he had a plan brewing. They could head over to his condo. Once they could be alone and sit across from one another, face to face, he could further assess her feelings. If she didn't care for him, he needed to know.

Although, between her second trip to the bathroom and another box of thin mints from concessions, Samentha was having issues with her allergies. She has these very specific fits during which she sneezed four or five times in a row, and after handing her some tissue, Steve tried one last, pathetic move, hoping that she couldn't resist him by then—he reached over, took the used tissue out of her hand, and placed his palm into hers.

For about a minute she didn't budge. But as the film played on, she began to feel emotionally overwhelmed. Who was this man, anyway? she asked herself. And why should she get involved with the first guy who seemed interested? She had to be more picky; Nora needed a father figure whom Sam could herself respect, and one whom she actually wanted to fall in love with.

But why don't I want this? she asked herself. Did she always refuse love when it was available? There are so many questions one asks oneself, when that vulnerable sensation begins to stir.

She felt awkward on their way up to his condo, almost avoiding his eyes completely. Sleeping with another man, someone other than John. .

.was she ready for it? And what if she got pregnant again? For a moment though, she wished she could be a completely different person than she had become. She was so protective and didn't always understand why she'd hold onto these feelings for so long. But, if she was uninterested in Steve, the way she framed it, she wouldn't be going back to his condo. She had one rule, though—that she would make it back home no later than 10:30, to put Eleanor to bed, and to get a decent amount of sleep herself.

Steve's condo was a high-rise in Brentwood overlooking the ocean, and for years he'd had fantasies of falling in love while looking out at that view, the way the traffic lights danced along to the sounds of children down by the pier. He had never really been in love with Kathy, but they'd shared some mornings at his condo that were pleasant. Perhaps that's why he didn't feel that he wanted to pick up his life and start over in Denver. But Kathy was part of his past now. And Santa Monica was such a delight on a cool February night.

Was Samantha impressed by Steve? On my end, it didn't seem likely. But this evening, she did try and convince herself that she could love him, or at least distract herself with the idea of love itself. Steve's humble abode had been updated with amenities that she didn't have at her own place. His entire home was spotless, which she didn't expect either. In the fridge he kept an assortment of rich cheeses and spreads with various berries, and he ate modestly and healthier than most men. She was impressed with this, though she was more a burger- and-fries kind of girl. She recalled how John loved his pickles on the side of his plate, and a little coleslaw with no mayo. *Oh John, why did you have to go and leave me*? ran through her head every time she thought about getting close to another man.

She certainly *liked* Steve.

But he seemed a bit immature for his age, although he was successful in his career, well-renowned, and respected. She liked the way he always made sure his shoes were tied, and his eyes seemed always to be searching for a tune floating around in his subconscious. And when he found one, he'd start humming along, gabbing on and on about how he and she were going to make this incredible album, dueling pianos, as a tribute to Smetana. Although he had confessed to her once that he secretly wanted to make the tribute to Tori Amos, and his lifestyle definitely suggested he was better off than Sam had anticipated. He was a lot of fun to be around. Crude, in a way. But not kind and gentle like me, she had come to realize over time.

Why couldn't she be more like Steve, she wondered, and just jump into new ideas, jump into the arms of love? She had to protect Nora, and with time she would know what to do, and who to be. But we all know what happens when you resist, when you decide to ignore the inevitable. If you ask me, I think Sam could do better. But I'll let you find out whether that assumption plays out in the end, as I must tend to young Eleanor now—no more time for worrying about or foretelling their future. Little Nora wants to so badly make brownies tonight, with walnuts, which I've never been fond of myself, but she teaches me new things each day. . .

"White wine, or red?" asked Steve, as he turned on the radio by the French windows and the lamp above his baby grand. He swayed back and forth, twirling and stomping his feet on the carpeted cement floors, making his way to the wine rack.

"Got any gin?" she replied, shyly, as her feet caressed the soft blue shag carpet.

"My lady, my lady—I am not a hard liquor kinda guy. But for next time, I'll remember. So what'll it be?"

"Red sounds nice. It has more antioxidants in it and less sugar. God knows I've had enough sugar tonight, all those thin mints."

"And the silent one has a voice after all! Now, tell me, what is it that's troubling you? Was the film so terrible? Is it my breath? It's my breath, isn't it?"

"No, it's not your breath, silly."

"Well, *something's* going on in there." He sat down next to her on the leather sofa. She complained about it feeling sticky, and that black would never be a color she'd choose for a couch, and how she wanted to change her hair. He listened, and after about fifteen minutes of indulging her, he put his arm around her and stared into her uncertain eyes.

One kiss, he thought, to seal the deal. One to swoon her so, and bewilder her senses—and that, finally, they could allow the enchantment to commence. No more waiting, no more awkward moments. Could this be it—entwined in a sensual manner there on his couch, or on the kitchen table, or the balcony? He moved in on her slowly, listening, consoling, giggling, staring deeper, touched her hair, and she let him.

And then he went for the kiss. As you might imagine, she didn't wish it one bit and pushed him away before she could get a taste.

"Sam, I don't understand! I'm not sure if you've forgotten about this, but I'm not seeing anyone else right now. And maybe that feels like pressure on your end? I want to be real here. I don't want to hurt you in any way. But I don't like wasting time."

"Is this wasting time, getting to know me?" She stood up, walked over to the piano, and played a few keys. She sat down at the bench, facing the view out to the ocean.

"Of course not," he said, holding back what he really wanted to say. "That's not what I meant." But why resist? Maybe they were just not right for each other. Could it be that she needed someone more docile, like herself? Kathy's ghost would sure be laughing at him in this moment—that he'd thrown away their relationship in order to court some single mom with no libido.

"Hey, Steve—I, uh, I move slow. I thought about this a lot during the film. And I don't know what I want exactly. I still think of John every morning. I have to be cautious for Eleanor. And Joseph, well, he's become a big part of her life, and I just. . . ."

"Please. Spare me. I want the truth. I won't stand for anything else," he pleaded, sitting in silence for a second. But then, "No, this isn't right, Sam. You don't look at me the same way you look at Joseph. And in fact I'm a bit jealous of that whole situation."

But though it was a great moment for them to truly open up with one another, she sat there holding her wine glass in both hands, saying nothing at all.

She was attracted to him, yes. But not yet *attached*, not in the way she was with me. She wasn't interested in me *sexually*. But I made her feel alive, seen, so comfortable in her life, in her skin, and with Eleanor. Steve had a long way to go in that department. All she could do was stare at his shadow behind him on the wall. Then she watched the lights dance far off on Santa Monica Boulevard, the Ferris Wheel on the pier. February's deepened breeze enraptured her, through the balcony doors and French windows. Even with Steve's arms around her, she felt no such warmth.

"Will you play me a song on your piano, Steve?"

"No. It's too late, the neighbors wouldn't appreciate it." He sat there a bit smugly, not afraid to show his disappointment any longer, but wishing that he had taken my advice, let go of his expectations, get to know her, at her pace. But why? So he could move in closer with her? It made no sense.

"Jealous of an old man, are you, Steve? If you're so interested in my being a part of your life, why not spend more time with my daughter? Make an effort. You want these lips? You want love, for real? The real fucking thing? Then make a real move! I don't want all these things, I don't care about this view, or your really nice blue carpet that's very clean and appears to be vacuumed recently. . .but no, I just—I don't care for wine, or some movie, I want family time. I am *broken*, Steve. And you just got out of a relationship."

"Wow. Okay. I didn't. . .well, see, I wasn't prepared to, I didn't know you were gonna bring up Kathy. And, geez, well, maybe I am jealous and rightfully so."

"You could show up once in a while just to see Nora, bring her something sweet. By now, you should know what she likes. It's not me you have to impress, it's her. If you can't see that, then I don't know what else to say to you." She finished what she had to say, and he sat on the couch below her, red-faced and completely made a fool of. But he deserved it. She was right. He *hadn't* done much to advance his connection with Nora; all he was thinking about was his discomfort feeling lost after his breakup with Kathy. . .and being lost in Samentha's sparkling eyes. He got up, poured them each a glass of water, and asked her if she wanted to use the bathroom before he drove her home. She agreed, and he went back into the kitchen.

He stood there for what felt like forever, waiting for the sound of the bathroom sink running, a flush of the toilet. But he heard nothing after she closed the door behind her. And, instead of waiting any longer, he played a bit on his piano.

She eventually came out of the bathroom. She was a mess. He could see that she'd been crying, but he kept playing and didn't look at her any longer. For a minute, standing there by the balcony, looking out again into the black sky as if a shadow of her past was always waiting around to haunt her, she listened to him play. It was the sky John had died in—that ugly, awful sky. She made her way to the other side of Steve's condo now, walking right past him as he continued to brood at the keys of his piano. She stood silently by the front door, staring into the opposite direction, where Steve was. He eventually got up from the bench, grabbed his keys, and walked down to the car with her.

It was 9:24 on a night in late February, the worst day of his life in a long while, because Kathy had never really mattered much to him. He'd wanted her to be part of his future, had convinced himself of it. But the only star he could see in his galaxy was this Samentha girl. He knew he had a lot of growing up to do, to show her that he could care for her daughter. But they said little on their drive back to her place. When she got out of the car, she didn't bother to turn around, not even to smile or wave goodbye. He watched her disappear into the lobby. But he didn't drive away just yet. He sat there, imagining how she might run back to his car, kiss him deeply, apologize, and move on to the next stage in their relationship. Why couldn't that be the case?

"HEY, GOOD-LOOKING! WHERE'S THE OTHER HALF?" I called out to a sour-faced Samentha. She looked just beside herself.

"Oh, he's downstairs in his car, probably sulking. He'd better drive off soon. I don't want any bit of that man around me in my space, energetically, whatever you wanna call it. I'm done."

"Done? So soon? The whole thing, it's over?" I felt relieved. God, Steve had to be a mess. I wondered how well he had taken my advice, if he had yelled at her—that ass-mouth of his had to be tamed. But then when I saw her face, and how distraught she was, I wonder instead, what had I done? Had I messed up a nice connection for them? Sometimes I am so stubborn, what a jerk-off. Here I was, hogging this woman's daughter; I was as much to blame for this whole thing.

"He kissed me," she said.

"Kissed you?" I was surprised, but I kept that to myself.

"Yeah. . .I panicked. I-I feel like I'm in this cocoon. So safe and protected from feeling anything at all. Of course, I feel things. I just don't let them get the best of me. He's a good guy, right?"

"Steve is one of my best friends. There *is* something I noticed about him when we first met. Years ago. He has this spark, and it's something that's always been missing from my life. I get stuck in my own head, I overthink, and I miss out on opportunities. Steve has an ability to really unleash the childlike part of me. Like how I feel when I'm with Eleanor—he makes me feel that way. But he does have a temper. And that is his downfall, yes. But he cares about you."

"He's got a lot to learn," she said, standing there by the rhododendron plants, picking off dead leaves, throwing the leaves onto the floor below her, crumbling some of them and sprinkling them into the air above her as she stared off into nothing.

"Steve is learning. But don't we all have a lot to learn, Sami?"

"Joseph?" she said, making her way towards me. She wasn't looking at me, not in my face, but in my general direction.

"What's that?"

"Will you hold me, just for a minute?" she said, almost in a burst of tears, and I quickly reached over to wrap my arms around her, completely engulfing her, as if I was holding a child. And she wept there in my arms.

Young Eleanor entered the room at once, eyes half-open, her blanket in one hand and a tattered, rosy-eyed doll in the other. I leaned down for a moment to pick her up and leaned back into Samentha. We put the sleepy girl to bed, returned to the living room, and continued to talk. I confessed to her that I felt this closeness I couldn't describe, but that it was there—not in a romantic sense, but that I knew I had to protect both of them. I even admitted how my life had more meaning with them in my life. She had a similar confession, and said that she felt ever so lucky to have felt so welcomed into a situation that none of us, not even Nora, could put a label on. Sometimes we need people in our lives, even if we don't know why everything has lined up the way it has. I don't believe in fate, and Sami certainly didn't. I figured there must be another word for it.

"Tell me about work," I said, to change the subject. "Mix things up a little. How has the transition been from your last spot up north?" That's what my grandmother used to do in these situations: Talk it out, then take a breather.

"I guess I'm still adjusting. To the hospital. It's fine."

"Do you like the nurses working under you? Are they. . .at least competent?" We laughed for a minute, then continued. . .

"I mean, they say that this children's hospital is one of the best facilities, both in their methodologies for treating patients as well as their benefits for staff. But this is a promotion for me. . . ." She started to untie her hair and removed her lipstick with her palm.

"Ah, that's right—you're the big boss now who's making quite a pretty penny, Steve tells me."

"In the past—and stop me if I'm repeating anything, by the way—in the past I was in charge of the first floor's antics. At this new spot I'm running the entire department. It's a huge responsibility. We keep getting babies from ICU out on the first floor, and there's just no room for errors there, Joseph. But the director, she's an older woman. And I feel like I've been learning a lot from her already. I think this is her third hospital. She's been here the longest—seventeen years now."

"What about the other staff?"

"Hm. I guess, yeah, you can say at this point I'm working two night shifts a week, which isn't so terrible. I need to get to know the night nurses, and this is the only way. But soon I'll get a chance to omit the late nights and focus instead on the day shifts."

"You're resilient, Sam."

"Thank you. I don't feel it. But I'm getting used to the whole thing. So tell me—I didn't want to bring this up, but I might as well."

"I'm an open book. But it is getting close to my bedtime as well."

"Yes, how silly of me. And I'm just exhausted. But real quick, I just wanted to say that I do hope your Abigail isn't getting the wrong impression, like how Steve is all hung up on our connection."

"Abi is. . .she's Abi! Suspicious, but very easy to talk to. She likes to get to the point, and I like to dream a little. So we work through our differences."

"Tell me again how you two met."

I told her all about that night we met, when Abi was right around Sam's age—how we'd stayed at the Ambassador that night, with me on the sofa. "Steve was there—he remembers our first night. She was so direct and confident in a way I just wasn't used to. As a woman, that is. We were both a bit boozed up, but I didn't take advantage of her. She thought I reminded her of Paul Newman and Brando! And the next morning. I'd never had a woman pursue me the way she did."

We continued like this for another hour or so. She told me a bit about how she'd met John. The way he wore his tie... always tucked into his jacket. And when he wasn't dressed up to please others, he was actually quite a casual guy. He had this purple pair of swim trunks that he'd bought one summer, and he made sure that, when Sam and Eleanor picked up their next swimsuits, they were in a similar hue.

John liked the simpler things in life. For breakfast, he liked cottage cheese and blueberries, whereas Sam and Nora wanted the works—ham and eggs, pancakes with maple syrup, and crisp bacon.

He didn't brood much, had no extended lamentations. He was a man who had no regrets and didn't mind if plans changed at the last minute. He was more of a plant person than Samentha, as he'd studied botany when he was younger. His mother was a great lover of oak trees and had a lovely vegetable garden.

But it was getting late, and Sam had to pack in the morning for her big trip up north.

I asked to see a photograph of John before I headed back to my place. I assumed there was a place where she had photographs of them all together. But the truth was, she kept all her relics of him, and of their relationship, packed away in a box. To be sorted through eventually, she told me. When the time felt right.

"GOOD MORNING, OLD MAN! DID I WAKE YOU?" said the voice, exuberant as usual, on the other end of the receiver. It was Steve, of course. I had yet to hear his side of the story. So, instead of floating around our usual dialogues on compositions for the piano and my complaints about my new comforter, I got right in there and pried. I figured it was going to be a longer conversation than I was ready for, especially so early in the morning. But it was 10:00 a.m. I'd slept in. That was quite rare—I never slept in that late, at least not all the way through. I had to get my day started. But I allowed for Steve's rambling while I got dressed, made my coffee, brushed my teeth, and rummaged through the weeds on the balcony plants.

"To tell you the truth, Joseph, she was nearly impossible last night. I felt like I was tucked back into the high school days. I felt like a complete idiot. I couldn't read her, and anytime I thought it was the right moment she resisted."

"Are you sure you're not behaving like an adolescent? I know how you get."

"Did she come to see you?. . . She talked to you already, didn't she? This is just too much. I mean, okay, I'm not gonna get upset. I gotta change here. Okay. Give it to me. She hates me, doesn't she?"

"Well, Steve, I, um, I think that maybe I shouldn't be in the middle here. I don't know if it'll be helpful for either of you. If she's resisting, then you give her what she wants. Resist her. And see how long she can take it."

"Resist her? Like, don't make any advances?"

"No. Nothing. If she wants to take it slow, give her what she asks for. If you were a single dad, and your wife had just died tragically, and *you* were starting your life over. . . ."

"You're right. I'm being a pig. God dammit, Joseph, you're a genius."

"Look, I think that you're still a bit jaded from Kathy."

"Yeah. You're probably right. Maybe I should have just followed her up to Denver. I always do that. I let go too soon. Such an idiot."

"Don't say that. She wasn't right for you. But you're growing now. It's the best we can do as humans. We change, we discover new things, patterns. But you do, as I've said to you before. . .you really need to establish a sort of empathy for women. They're not objects. There are things called compromise. We all have to make them. Abi likes having separate spaces, and I want to be with her--so we have our separate spaces. Do I wish we lived together in the same home? Yeah. I do. But I believe one day we'll get there."

"Don't hold your breath, though. How do you know she doesn't have someone on the side? Especially with all of her traveling?"

"Do you really think she's got one dishonest bone in her body?"

"I guess not. Abi adores you. But how long are you guys gonna play this silly game with the different places? You're both going to need each other on a deeper level one of these days. What if Abi falls down in the kitchen, and there's no one there? You could be off taking the ladies over here out for ice cream when your actual girlfriend might actually need you. Maybe the reason why she doesn't want to live with you is that you're not making the effort to show her that's what you want."

"Maybe I do need to talk to her about that. Yeah. I hear you, Steve. Abi was always the one with the balls to go for what she wanted. And I just sit at my piano and wallow, wondering when life will make more sense. But as I get older, I don't worry as much about certain things. And I've adjusted to my life here, without someone to hold each morning. It's not, it's just not—"

"You need someone too, Jack."

"Ha! Yeah. I miss Abi. Maybe I just miss what we were in the beginning. Maybe I'm too lazy, at this point, to care for more. But Eleanor, she fulfills me in that way. I feel needed."

"See, this is where we're good for each other. You're a pushover, you don't go for what you really want, and I put out too much effort into what I think I want. And, uh. . . ."

"And then when you get what you want, you discard it."

There was a long pause before he asked, "Is that what I do?"

"Yeah. But who am I to judge?"

"You can judge."

"I feel like we're in some stage play, and the audience hasn't revealed itself just yet. But there's a child in the distance, laughing. Laughing at me, because I haven't realized it's just a stage. And if I walked off in the other direction, went into the dressing room, changed my shirt, smelled the perfume at the counter, climbed out the window and. . .and up the side of the veranda, maybe I'd enter in to another life, where I could make other choices."

"You just wrote our next song, Jack!"

"Oh, did I?" And oh, did I feel better talking to Steve. Sure he could be an ass, yet when we got to talk, things made a lot more sense.

But it was time for me to get on with my day. We agreed that I needed to be more honest with Abigail, and that Steve needed to slow down with Samentha.

"And just one more thing. . .you're both moving at a different pace, and this is good for you!"

"I know, I know."

"So, if you don't mind my saying, you might want to think about measuring your commitment to Samentha from a different perspective. Through your prism, it's short-sighted. Your insecurities kick in if she isn't ready for a kiss. You take it to mean she isn't interested—in the same way you interpreted Kathy's move to Denver as a means to escape the relationship. These women aren't in the business of giving you constant reassurance, and you're not to seek these endeavors as proof of their love for you."

"I dunno. You put your arms around Sam way too often for me to be comfortable with. How do you explain your lack of restraint with her?"

"As I told you before, she's all alone with that little girl. I never had a daughter, and I regret that every day I wake up. Take it or leave it. That's me."

"I'll take it!"

"Alright, then," I muttered, laughing as I poured a second cup of coffee. Today I had to go for a run, then to the gym, post office, and once again I'd stop by the market to pick up a few things; batteries, rubber bands, Post-It notes, cat food (the wet kind, for the kittens downstairs below the balcony).

"Jo, yo, I've got to get to a hearing in Van Nuys. Thank you for, you know, talking to me. I didn't want to put you on the spot. But I think you knew this was coming."

We hung up, and I kept thinking about, well, again, why I was even putting myself in the middle in the first place.

I wondered if my first wife was still alive these days. I could imagine her drinking herself to death. She had such great hair, much thicker than Abi's. And then I was thinking about all the women I've been with. Even back before my wife, all those girls I slept with in the early Seventies, before I went to university. There was Ingrid, who had blonde hair and brown eyes but no ass. She could cook: that was quite something. One night, our second day together, she made me vegetable lasagna, and I hadn't tasted anything so delicious my entire life. Her breath always smelled of rosemary, and her tits were like pennies. But we had a weekend that I held onto for a while, out there, fighting and flying.

And then there was Janice, who had two kids already. We slept together out on a rock one morning; her two boys were in summer camp, and I had stopped in her small town around 4:00 a.m. We locked eyes at a deli, went for a hike, and afterwords I walked her back to the deli and never saw her again.

Then there were all the women whose names I never got. What if I was just as cruel a father as Samentha's own mystery sperm donor? Is this my connection, my guilt, that I must have knocked up one of those women, and that's why my ex-wife was such a nightmare? That it was my karma for being an asshole, like most men who are raised to perform.

So then who am I to advise Steve on his shithead ways of how he treats women? I've done the same thing. Maybe that's why Abi won't live with me. Could it be that it's not so exact that she wants her own space, but that I'm impossible to be around?

I felt badly then, as if the whole encounter with Nora and her mother was a way to rub the past in my face. If I had known that I had a daughter with one of those women, way back when, would I have run away? How can a man be forgiven for abandoning his own child? How does that make Samentha feel? She tells me, but I don't know what the feeling is. She once described it to me as being like a prisoner who has served forty so odd years, for no reason. How do you give back forty years of fully lived life without a father around? No amount of compensation can repair that damage. I can't go back. I can't change any of it.

All those years—a total loss: And to think that I could be one of those cruel fathers. That I may have taken that away from a girl just like Sami. Is Nora waiting for her father to return? She talks to him sometimes when I'm around, too. She doesn't hide it well, and Sam is suspicious of how healthy that could be. And how painful it is to watch her daughter grow up without a father, just like she did. But there are no photographs of John around the house, and none of Sam's father, either—no face to see in your dream, only a total darkness, a measure of uncertainty following you like a shadow; it's only a shadow, and it will always follow me.

CHAPTER SIX

700 FLYERS

MICHAEL'S WAS A QUASI-LUXURY RESTAURANT located off Rodeo Drive, and housed a rather prodigious courtyard for its patrons —mainly locals, my neighbors and their families, since the tourists preferred crummier areas—I'd been fascinated by Sunset Blvd when I first moved here myself. There's something charming about the smell of urine and celebrity sightings that makes for a unique story. Many of our passersby come from Germany and France; some even hail from Portugal. I've never been to France, but Abi ventures there often. Without me, of course.

Regardless, since the Nineties this unassuming bistro has become a bit of a sanctuary for the public, and when I introduced it to Samentha, she had become attached almost immediately. I've noticed that my suggestions tend to stick with that one. Often, Michael's was where she met her close friends—particularly a gal named Sandra, with whom she'd been working most recently.

Today, the two women are meeting for breakfast after a tumultuous night shift at the hospital. Kvetching always comes first as they gaze out amid others finishing up a plate of hash browns and pancakes deluxe. Although Sam never orders them, she likes to imagine them being made on the grill, then brought over to someone else's table, at which she will gaze, breathe in deeply, and remain enamored by the whole experience. It was something she did as a child, she once told me; "hotcake gawking" is what she actually calls it. These childlike endeavors she engages in give me an inexplicable feeling of closeness, one that often overwhelms me. But before I get too carried away, let's allow for the ladies to have their breakfast. . . .

"So, tell me Sam, is it just me, or is Dr. Ginsburg a real prick?" Sandra began, almost spoiling the moment, but Sam leapt up in her seat to respond appropriately.

"Tell me about it. He can be a real son of a bitch. But that's how it goes, right? With those types, emotionally unavailable, hot-headed. . .I just shrug it off. But, hey, if there's anything I can do in one of my departments, I take suggestions, ya know." She offered her condolences as well.

"Maybe I'm just getting too old for this type of work. I don't have the patience I used to. And I'm sick of working around people like him. And it's not just a male thing either— there are plenty of women on my floor who just don't give a rat's ass about doing their job. They have no passion for helping people. Makes me sick."

Sandra unfolded her napkin, placed it on her lap, sighed quite loudly, and looked over her shoulder to the rather loud children sitting at the table behind her. Might she never catch a break from this aberration?

"Yeah, I've been feeling that way too lately. Kind of sick of it all makes sense, if I really sit down and analyze the bigger picture. It's like people don't care about one another anymore. But yeah. . .alright, so what happened exactly with Dr. Ginsburg?"

"He came in at 5:00 a.m., and he was checking the chart of the seven-week-old baby. Leslie was standing next to him when he turned and barked, 'You gave her *three* milligrams instead of *two.* Idiot! Can't you follow my instructions?'

"'I did *not* give her three milligrams,' she shot back, shivers shooting down her small frame.

"'Here! Read it for yourself!'

"'But it's impossible. I did *not* overdose her.'

"'It's on the *chart*, is it not? Didn't you write that?'

"'No!'"

"'Then who the hell recorded the dosage on the chart?'

"'Rose did. I was dictating to her what to record, and she put it down.'

"By that time," Sandra continued, "Rose'd entered the room accompanied by me, and the doctor repeated the accusation. Rose, half frozen, claimed that she'd recorded the dosage based on what she heard Leslie call out. I stepped in and decided to resolve the issue before it got out of hand, and I asked Leslie to retrieve the vial from the patient's file at the store room. The protocol, as you know, is to keep the vials on hand for one week after use.

"She returned with the vial that showed two milligrams. It turned out that Rose had misheard Leslie and recorded three milligrams. Thank God we keep the evidence for a week. I asked Rose to have her ears checked, and Dr. Ginsburg stood there feeling naked and cold. 'I apologize for my choice of words,' he said, 'and I'm glad that this has cleared up. I was worried!'

"Another fire put out at 5:00 a.m. where days and nights are indistinguishable."

"You've got something else to tell me, don't you?" Sandra whispered, handing Sam her pen and notebook. "Look, write it down if you can't say it. I do that with my son. When he feels it's too hard to say something, he's scared of hearing it out loud. Whatever it may be. So we've got this thing going where I hand him a piece of paper, and I tell him, when he's ready, he can write it down. And he can come to me with the paper, and

I'll read it to myself. And then, I let him talk it out."

"You have some profound methodologies there."

"It's part of why I'm such a catch."

"You're a good mother. That's not always the case."

"You're divine. Alright, spill it. What else is ticking behind those emerald green eyes?"

"Los Angeles is a complicated place, Sandra. I miss John. And even if he's not around, at least when I was in Oregon I still felt his presence."

"He hasn't been gone very long."

"You're a doll." Samentha sat there and thought about the very last time she saw John and Nora together, sitting back in their sailboat, light green sails somewhat transparent, up at Crater Lake. It was where Eleanor first encountered nature's glory and inherent unkindness, the first time she learned how to read. They were out on the boat, counting the ripples that would pulse from out the cockpit. The wooden hull was painted light blue, and there was a discussion about how, when Nora turned seven, they would celebrate by letting her decide how to paint the boat the following spring. The girl with the pink glasses made a list of what she would draw: roses, scissors, boots, a baby elephant, a few ruby-red strawberries. But that day never came for them.

"Sandra?"

"Yes?"

"I was thinking if, in the near future, I moved back to Oregon. . .would you think I was completely ridiculous?"

"You're really someone I look up to. And I'm not shitting you there. You're imaginative, motivated, and very realistic when it comes to making changes."

"You think so? I mean I just got here. . . ."

"I'm not one to tell you what to do. But Los Angeles is complicated. Even when it's lovely, there's nothing like a real community, affordable living, maybe even breathable air. Those things just don't exist in this place."

"Thank you. I needed to hear all that."

"Don't mention it. Oo, here comes our food." They eyed the delicacies: sunny-side-up eggs, a hamburger patty and the works on a whole-wheat roll with butter and some jam on the side. They always ordered the same thing, as these silly traditions made up a huge part of their friendship. They often coordinated their socks for shared shifts at the hospital, and when the night got rough and they spotted one another on the other side of the hospital, Sam would pull up her pant-legs and flash Sandra her electric green socks. And Sandra would do the same. At times they'd even coordinate sack lunches, and it would make the other nurses jealous at times. They enjoyed this game, if that's what you could call it.

It was something that they needed at that moment in their lives. . .to feel understood, to have something in common. Sandra's husband was so drastically different from her, there just weren't many things for them to relate on. At their core, in the marriage, there were values missing, dreams that they didn't share, sex never to be had: Affection was not exactly a part of their relationship. It made Samentha sad to discover Sandra's ball-and-chain dilemma. Having someone to hold and caress is so essential to making a partnership work. It's about the synergy, not just the sacrifices. In fact, too many sacrifices can spoil the whole thing. Resentment is never pretty.

Sandra and her man were miles apart. Kind of like Abi and me, at times. Well, ever so recently. We just don't see eye to eye, although we didn't start off that way. Oh, Abi, how did we mess this up? I wondered what she was up to that moment—filing her nails out on her patio, listening to the radio, and secretly eavesdropping on the neighbors during the commercial breaks. Abi never cared much to over-indulge in the news, but she was aware of the happenings across the airwaves. I, on the other hand, I obsess at times.

But where was I. . .oh, yes, Sandra and Sam, gloating about work-related fallacies, life epiphanies, and stuffing their faces with breakfast. Sandra had revealed that, as a matter of fact, her husband had gone on and on about how they couldn't afford to go on their annual trip to their favorite spot in the South--Eureka Springs, Arkansas, where they'd met ten years back, so they would fly each anniversary to their old stomping grounds and spend a week sitting by the river, visiting old friends, and paddle-boarding and live music came into the mix.

This year, it wouldn't happen. He had told her that they needed to save up for "more important things" like their retirement plan and perhaps a new car. But he wasn't being completely transparent. And Sandra was deeply disappointed when she discovered in their bank records that he had secretly purchased a one-bedroom condo in Greece. She hadn't brought it up, but she wasn't surprised—could be dishonest. The red flags were always there; the question is whether we're prepared to acknowledge them.

Have we all lost sight of what it means to be together? Relationships should be re-built regularly, but how? I mean, Abi and I weren't exactly married. Maybe I should have proposed to her already. I guess I was waiting for her to do it. Is it too late now? Do we break up, or take the next step? I could meet someone new. . .why not? But a breakup is complicated. Some call it the fear of being alone. That big "what happens next?" although everyone I've met who's left a partner and performed the hard work and discipline required for such a transition discovers an abundance of opportunities that arrive when they made the conscious decision to better their life—to find someone who *gets* them, someone they're compatible with. It does exist. People like to make excuses for staying miserable. So it may very well be that people *are* afraid to find true love Iand just settle. Of course they do. So why not let go of someone who could also do much better, without the dreaded attachment to a relationship that never really worked.

I'm really talking more about Sandra and her husband. Abi and I had it good for a while. But I pretended to blame her for the dilemma of living apart. I was scared of our connection. Why did I push her away? We never *fought*—perhaps an argument here and there.

The work that it takes to get out of a marriage is often what prevents couples in a loveless situation from separating. But eventually love prevails, and one or the other will move on to brighter horizons.

But I'm getting carried away here. What's going on with Sandra and Samentha? Let us return to their quaint breakfast antics, more or less a coming together of two lost doves on their way to the watering hole.

"So tell me Sam, what's going on aside from missing John?" Sandra took another generous sip of coffee. She had dropped a few bits of egg onto her blouse, but no matter, she was off work now, time to get messy.

"Did I ever tell you about growing up without knowing who my biological father was?" Samentha leaned in closer to her friend, chewing open-mouthed with eyes of pink and hazel, hints of viridian.

"Your father. . .vaguely."

"It's like this dark cloud over my head for the last, I dunno, thousand years or so." Sam began to tear up but held it back. She started to cut up her eggs with a fork and push them to the side of the plate, pouring a little too much hollandaise sauce over her wheat-roll. She tasted the sauce with her pinky, looking up to Sandra, awaiting her response.

"A thousand years? Good lord, that's a long time."

"Yeah. . .like, I wonder, is he alive still? Does it even matter? Wouldn't it be nice for my Nora to know her grandfather? Just so many questions that keep coming to me, at night, in the morning—I mean, fuck it, all *day*. Especially since John's been gone."

"Why hold it all in? What's the point?"

"As far back as I could bury these feelings, I did so, for most of my life. Sometimes, what we want is so frightening that we push it away. As if, if I could pretend long enough, and I could keep that up, it would eventually go away. How long could I numb myself? But life doesn't work like that, not exactly. I learned this from my daughter. There were so many things I was oblivious to until I gave birth to her and got to discover how incredible life could be if I just took the time to see the world through her eyes. Unless we fully deal with something, face it for what it is, it'll never go away."

"I know. I know."

"I kept the whole thing stored in the back of my mind, shoved at the tiniest pathetic crevice in my heart. Even in my relationship with John, I never brought it up. I was afraid he'd judge me, or I'd get lost in the feeling and lose interest in him altogether. He wasn't always around much anyways, being overseas so often."

". . .I don't want you to hide your father any longer. You can be vulnerable with me. I'm not going to judge you. I give you permission to give yourself permission to. . .um, let it be what it is."

And as soon as Sandra finished speaking, Sam broke down into tears, sobbing as if she had just seen a ghost from her past. Sandra leapt out of her chair and went over to hold her, and wept a bit as well. Tears are meant to be shared sometimes. If only men could be that real. As an emotional man myself, I always felt that I could relate more to women. But I always kept up my masculine ways as if to trick others, so they wouldn't recognize me.

Sam calmed down, splashed her face with some ice water, laughed a bit, and took off her shoes as she looked around at the other tables, and for a second she was. . .what was that strange aroma? Almost like smoke, coming from behind her. She turned toward a brown-eyed vixen sitting by the bougainvillea, smoking something she'd never seen before.

"It's called a 'clove,' hon," the twenty-something said when she asked her. "They kinda crackle when you take a hit. They're absolutely spectacular. I like to smoke them before I go to bed, but it's often hard for me to resist right after breakfast. Want one? It'll cost ya."

"Oh. Are they very expensive?"

"Nah, just tell me your name. We'll call it a deal."

"My name?"

"Yeah."

"It's, uh, it's Samentha. But Mama calls me Junebug at times."

"I like that. June buggy Sam. Well, enjoy your clove, my dear. I'm off to work now, see you around maybe."

"Thank you! Uh, do you have a light by any chance?" Sam placed the slender, black cancer-stick into her mouth, which she hadn't done since she was twelve years old. The full-figured, sassy girl with the pearly teeth lit her clove and waved a casual farewell motion as she made her way off toward the parking lot.

Sam wandered out the door. "You enjoying that?" Sandra asked, holding her cup of coffee close to her chin, taking little sips as she swatted at a mosquito.

"It's actually quite smooth. Almost like a cigar. Mm. Did you want to try some?" They stood leaning over the fence, watching the clouds move quickly across the horizon.

"Did you still want to talk about your father?"

"Yeah, I can do that."

"You know his name?"

"No. I know nothing. But, when I moved back to Los Angeles, Joseph, you know—"

"That sweet older gentleman who Nora has taken a liking to."

"Yeah. He, well, he was telling me that when he was in the Israeli Air Force, as a flyer, he once wanted to research who in his family had actually survived the Holocaust. You know, it was believed that very few *had* survived the death camps in Poland. So Joseph got in touch with this Swiss organization—I guess they take a sample of your blood and try and match your DNA with someone else's close to that bloodline in your family."

"I got mine done a decade ago. It was wild."

"Were you nervous?"

"Well, maybe a little. I didn't wanna find out if someone in my family had been at the helm of some horrific event, afraid I'd feel struck by unnecessary guilt. But it turned out to be helpful. Especially for my son, when they do those assignments where the kids have to talk about their family history? It'd be good for your daughter."

"I don't know. Maybe I don't want to *know* who my father is?"

"It's nice to know a name at least, right?"

". . .I think so. I'd like to know his name."

"Talk to more people about it. I'm sure that at least half of ones in your apartment complex have had the test done. Just go door to door or something. Even better, leave a little note at everyone's doorstep. That could be fun for Nora, too."

"Actually, I do know someone already who's had the DNA test done."

"There you go!"

"It was kind of miraculous, actually—he discovered an uncle, his mom's brother, who after the war moved to Belgium thinking that no one in his family was left. Which was almost, like, thirty years after the war. So that gave me a lot of hope. And curiosity, ya know?"

"I believe that I was able to have it narrowed down to about a hundred people that matched my DNA, and it goes globally, Sam."

"You're right. I shouldn't be so scared. This might be my only chance to put my mind at rest, something my mama failed to do. Or, I don't know, she may have been just as frightened as I was. She never wanted to talk about it. I'd ask her about him, and she'd reveal very little. It was as if she didn't care at all. Or that she didn't give a shit about what I wanted as her daughter. Why do people even have children if they can't do the necessary work? I would never for the life of me hold anything like that back from my Nora."

"Does she still speak with the dead?"

"Oh, that. God. I've been taking her to a child therapist. It's free through her elementary school, which is nice. But I don't want Nora to feel like she can't be herself. If she feels connected to John, that's her father. She can talk to him, I guess. Right? Am I. . .I just don't know exactly how to navigate around that. I want her to be happy, to feel that what she needs matters. Is she really talking to John's ghost? I just don't know."

"Well, then, this has been quite a heavy smorgasbord of, uh, breakfast topics. A lot to digest. Honey, I want you to take it easy, alright? One thing at a time. Let's get the DNA test done. You've got nothing to lose." Sandra took her friend's pale hand into hers and held it for a few seconds.

"Thanks, Sandra. You know, I appreciate you. My life hasn't been as light and smooth as I once anticipated."

They returned to their table. "And I'm sure working at the hospital makes everything even more stressful."

"I was thinking I should take a little break from work. Perhaps a trip."

AS THEY SAT DOWN TO FINISH THEIR BREAKFAST, I was pulling up to the semi-circular drive in front Abigail's house. It was close to 10:00 a.m., and the sun was out in full force, not a cloud in the sky. The palms that lined the street were swaying gently, then tenaciously for moments. It felt almost like spring had peeked it's head through the cypress trees, a slight protuberance of hope with the thought of various blooms opening on the veranda back at my place.

But I was going to spend some time with my Abi. There were so many birds that would come in season to this part of Los Angeles, some with long tails, others with high-pitched calls. The Charadrius vociferus, who nest in agricultural areas mainly, yet by Abi's place tend to gather within the stony substrates, urban rooftops, even hopping around the driveway. But the black phoebe is one of my favorites, the Sayornis nigricans, who tend to stay close to the water and rarely stray. . .although luckily for Abi and myself, they found the tiny man-made stream that runs through her backyard, and have nested there for quite a while. Abi says that they like to eat the grubs and Japanese beetles that come around during the early parts of summer. I have also always loved the color green, and luckily the Tachycineta thalassina has made its way to our neck of the woods, a violet-green swallow that nests in tree cavities, from the faraway muskegs of Alaska to the highlands in Mexico. Their birdsong is often mechanical, and they sound like they're mimicking the static song of the powerlines.

I rang the bell, and there she was, waiting for me at the door, smiling the way she does, in her house robe and slippers. She poured me some tea, since I had already had three cups of coffee. Self-improvement: Hey, I have to be careful I don't overdo it. My doctor has recommended I cut down on caffeine. Chocolate is fine, but eventually I'll need to narrow it down to just one to two cups of the luscious dark espresso that I often dream about upon waking.

Abi's backyard had the most delightful rose garden I'd ever seen, but she doesn't take all the credit. It was really the work of her gardener Jimmy, whom she always makes sure to send off with a kiss on his left cheek and a fresh bundle of roses to take home to his girlfriend. Jim lives just a few blocks down the street, and is close friends with Abi's sister Gale—who has been estranged from her for almost a decade now. But Jimmy comes around and takes care of Abi's blooming beauties, and fills her in on what's going on in Gale's life, whom he's been having an affair with, if she's healthy, where she's working, and if she's mentioned Abi. But Gale has never spoken one word about her sister. This has been hard for Abi to accept, but she's lived with it for so many years now. It's almost as if she never had a sister in the first place. I'm not one to make sense of this, though when she wants to talk about it, I let her. But I don't usually ask about Gale unless Abi brings it up first.

"Jack. . . ."

"Yes, love?"

"You know something funny? Two nights ago, I had a dream about the Ambassador. We were both drunk, and you were so cute. As gorgeous as I remember you. As gorgeous as you are now."

"Don't flatter me—I am not at all the hunk I used to be."

"Well, if you ask me, it's as if no time had passed at all."

"You're too good to me."

"No, I'm not. I could be a better girlfriend."

"Are you fishing for a compliment, or is something on your mind?"

"I'm, um, I dunno. The dream was just so *real*."

"Did I take advantage of you this time around?"

"No, you were just the same gentleman as you were when I first laid eyes on you. Even in my dreams, you're a sweetheart."

"Do you miss those days as much as I do? You know, staying out all night, a few unnecessary drinks—"

"It depends. Yes and no. I'd love to have more energy, like I used to. The late nights, those were quite something. As if we had all the time in the world. And now. . . ."

"And now?"

She sighed and moved the hair from off my brow, and kissed my forehead now, making sure my shirt was straight. "And now, well. . .do you still trust me after all these years?"

"Of course I do. What a silly question to ask."

"Next Sunday is our eighteenth anniversary! I just can't believe it. . .I hate how time gets away with so many things, and here I am trying to chase it down. And I look older each year."

"Oh, don't get me started. I feel like I keep noticing new creases that don't disappear on my arms after I lay them down a specific way. Sometimes I even think that, if I smiled less, I'd have less wrinkles, maybe, around my eyes and mouth."

"No. The world needs your smile. *I* need your smile."

"Abi—" I started hesitantly, and I should have just waited until later, but I can't keep my big mouth shut—"honey, there's something I wanted to talk to you about. And if now isn't the right time, then we can come back to it. I don't want to spoil this moment. But. . . ."

"Ah, I see. You're not just here for my love. There's a dilemma, isn't there? Steve broke Samentha's heart, and you must come to the rescue?"

"Well, actually it's the other way around. Sam has been refusing Steve's advances. She doesn't trust him, and I don't blame her. Plus he's on the rebound."

"It's his temper, really. I mean, Jack come *on*. The guy is ready to blow his top anytime someone has an opinion. He used to be so playful, and a great listener, too. But these days, or at least the last few years. . .he's been getting on my nerves. And what's happening with this album you two are working on? Didn't you start recording over a year ago? What's taking so long?"

"Steve doesn't always like to finish things when it comes to music. When it comes to love, he's all over the place. But look, it was something else I needed to talk to you about." I should have kept the focus on Steve, as I knew what I was about to say next would not launch be a pretty conversation.

"Abi. . . ."

"What is it, Jack?"

"I never really got to talk to you about something. It may surprise you, but in my defense, I guess, this realization didn't occur to me until, well—"

"Until she moved in."

Abi got it right away; she was always the intuitive one. That's what I loved about her. She could *read* me—I couldn't hide even if I had wanted to. I couldn't hide even if I had tried. She went on, "I knew this was bound to happen sooner or later. I can't say I'm surprised. So what do you have to say? You're in love with a woman twenty years your junior, and, well, what's the point of staying in this relationship with me when I'm off over here living my life—without you, quite often. And we both know we're miles apart. No matter the time that promised us something grand. The truth is, you'd probably be better off with her. You've always wanted a daughter."

"Now, don't go throwing *that* at me, Abi. I'm *not* in love with her. I'm not!"

"You and Steve, both of you letting your imagination get the best of you. It's just wrong. She could do much better than Steve. And you know it!"

"Abi. . .I don't think that you and I have ever talked about what I'm about to divulge. Again, this is not because I hid any information from you. It's just that this whole thing, what I'm about to tell you, has just come into focus. And it does involve Samentha. She awakens something inside of me, but it far surpasses love. It's a synchronicity that I can't explain, as it makes no sense to me, it just. . .it makes. . .I can't. . . ." I started to tremble a bit, which, although I am a sensitive sort of guy, was as if something had physically taken over my senses. Is it always this hard to follow one's desire for a life that makes more sense? Might I have sprung from my cocoon too swiftly? Or perhaps I had been sleeping much too long, and I've grown weaker from just waiting. . .and waiting.

"Hey, what's going on in there? In your head? You're just staring and mumbling. Earth to Jack!" Abi was getting impatient, and although she was quite graceful in that state, I know she was angry at me, furious, because she'd never let me in all the way, and I'd never let her. That's why we never moved in together.

I'd stayed with her because I thought it worked, and it did for a while—until I awoke from my final daydream dilemma, scorched by the arrival of winter and my avoidance of the piano. It'd been so long since I'd written a song. When I stopped feeling the drive to compose, I had known something was wrong.

Oh, God, she's *waiting*, I told myself. I need to *focus* here. "I have to tell you, Abi. Listen to me. When I first came to Los Angeles, it was 1970.

I'd met a few girls I had short encounters with. That was before I'd met my ex-wife back in the Northridge days."

"What the hell does this have to do with *Samentha*? Are you diverting?"

"No, I'm not *diverting*! I don't care if this doesn't make sense, I just need you to listen. Here's the thing: Sam's mother told her, sat her down when she was old enough to process things in this way, she revealed to her that there had been an Israeli flyer she was briefly involved with, and they'd lost contact."

Abi shook her head. ". . . Joseph, there were *thousands* of Israelis pouring into Los Angeles at that time, *thousands*. You know this—you're a numbers guy."

"But I was one of those seven hundred flyers in the late Sixties. There was just this one batch of men, which narrows down the pool who may have fathered Samentha. And if there were just four pilots who came into the port of Los Angeles that week I arrived, where do I fit in to that probability?"

"So she thinks—"

"*She* doesn't think anything of this, since I haven't said a word to her about it. She's carried a heavy grief, never knowing who her father was. And to think that one of those many women I slept with could have gotten pregnant—'cause, Abi, that's how things were in the Sixties. . . ."

"You don't have to *apologize*. The summer of love was each and every year for *me*. You know this, Joseph."

"Okay. Yeah. Well, the point is, I could very well have knocked up a few women. And to think of the pain that Sam carries with her, I could be responsible for that same awfulness that who knows how many women have experienced. I can't live with that. And helping her find her father feels like a way for me to somehow fix everything. Because I never had a child. It's been the one thing missing from my life. Almost as if I set myself up for this."

Abi took a deep breath. "Alright. I hear you. You feel free in this decision. It fits you. It's your choice. And I can't stop you from making it. We built a life together, but sometimes you have to let go of what you built. There are many stages in life. Some people are meant to be together for a certain amount of time, and maybe you and I are like passing ships?"

". . .I think you're right, Abigail."

"So, yeah. Alright. You gotta fix this, don't you?"

"I do. I need to."

"I understand, Jack. I can't say that I feel good about it. But I appreciate you telling me what's going on. What else? I know you've got more to say."

She came up to me and fussed with my hair for a minute. I took her hand and kissed it, then laid it against my cheek. She began to weep some, and I let her call me all the names she wanted to call me. Then we continued.

"If the population in Israel consisted of five million Jews in the Sixties," I murmured finally, "we—I mean the Israeli Air Force—represented, yes, a tiny fraction of the total. Yes, we were a rare animal, you could say, even to this day. But eight hundred soldiers took on that arduous course, and only forty-five of them graduated. So the chance that I slept with Sam's mother is extremely high!"

"Okay, I get it! And what? You gotta take a DNA test, don't you?"

"I suppose that's the next step."

"Well, I can't help you with that one."

"The thought that I have a child who remained fatherless is *killing* me. I'm going *mad*—not knowing who I am, or where I am for that matter. And do I even care to know these things? I don't know. It's incomprehensible to say the least, it keeps me up all night, and you're not there with me enough for me to feel like I shouldn't figure this whole thing out! You're not *around*, Abi! I want more than this. And you know that. No matter how I've protected myself, I've wanted more. From you.

But how can I blame you for my own foolishness? . . . I stuck around knowing that you couldn't provide me with something that you didn't have in the first place."

"I just wish you'd have told me, years ago, that you wanted something else. You know? Why did you wait so long?"

"I was *scared*, for Chrissake. I was scared."

"Yeah—well, I'd be scared for that poor girl, losing her husband, moving in next door to you. . .you're a mess, Joseph. You're a mess, and you know it. If you want more in life, then tell me what you want. I'll give it to you, if I can."

"'If I can' is *not* what I want. What I want has to be there already. I can't change you, nor can I alter my own true nature."

"This is so heavy. I'm shocked."

"Are you really?" I asked, knowing that she'd been lonely too in this relationship. And her jealousy of me having a kinship with children. . .her total being as this stubborn entity, one barely invested in relating to something outside of her travels and her stories, which were quite honestly a bore. This is quite a mess, I was thinking, isn't it?

"You can't undo things, Jack. That's not what you're good at. So swallow the pill and wash it down, my love. You're not going anywhere."

"Stop calling me Jack. My name is Joseph. And I can undo or redo anything I like. See, Abi, my dear, I've made up my mind. You can't talk me out of it. I don't care how cultured you say you are, or how ridiculous you think I'm being, or how beautiful the things we've shared have been. There is still something huge missing. And I'm going to claim it. Even if I have to risk my life along the way, I'm going to claim it. Samentha could have benefited from her father from the very beginning, and this is too much for me to bear."

". . .So then, where do you go from here? Isn't it truly her responsibility to figure all of this out? I mean, you're not expected to venture out and search for this trail of children that you may or may not have left behind along the way, are you? It's laughable. I'd like to see you actually go through with it. I really would."

I stood there and stared into her cold eyes for just a minute, tracing my mind with her disagreeable smirk, which seemed vile, pitiless, reptilian. Then I walked away from her, reconciled to the fact that she didn't see me. I walked away standing tall with no sense of defeat, and I wasted not another word on her. Because it was happening. Because it was unfeigned and real.

CHAPTER SEVEN

GLOBAL DNA CONNECTIONS

INTIMACY THROUGH CO-DEPENDENCY: Was that my dirty little secret? I had learned Abi wasn't exactly my soul mate; but I had been convinced otherwise for a long while. Perhaps I had violated the trust between us. Was it accidental self-sabotage? I'm a madman, I'd also come to conclude. What if Sam suddenly changed her mind, once she got to Oregon, about our connection. Not that we'd talked about it too often, but the subject had come up. We didn't have to even speak about it, it was just there, so what was I so worried about? Perhaps she was sick of me already, and I was just some daydreaming schmuck awaiting some answer to a question I was too afraid to ask. But I knew there was more to the story, aside from life-long misconceptions and woeful regrets. Abi never had any regrets, though, and for those lessons I guess you could say I'm grateful for her inhabiting my periphery for all those years.

It was Friday evening, and the dining table was set with the china I'd been holding onto—the remnants of mother's estate from many years back. My lady Rosa, the first gal I'd ever hired as a housekeeper, was at times more dependable than Abi, if you ask me.

Rosa was not only my housekeeper, she was also an awful singer. But she comes later in the day, so I have my mornings at least. I can't complain, though; Rosa has been a great motivator for getting me out of my head when I'm in those dark hours, brooding by the bay windows. She has an incredible adaptability that I'd never witnessed in my lifetime before I found her. She's a person you'd want on your side when the apocalypse hits. Aside from being my friend, and among her other household duties, she made sure the fridge was never empty, and going to the market had always been a bit of a drag for me. I'd rather stay at home and shave, or read the paper, then wander around the aisles in a daze, pushing those germ-covered shopping carts past all the products and their competitors' lined up on the shelves, as if waiting for an execution to take place. I can hear the train sounding its mighty call into the evening of what I can only describe as one of the longest days of the year.

Why, you ask? Well, I have yet to tell Samentha my idea about taking her and Eleanor to Oregon. I haven't given that much time to the thought, just the last forty-eight hours. I've even dreamt about our arrival, driving up to her ex's parents' home nuzzled away between the pine trees and drifting gray clouds with their auburn shadows.

Or so I imagine. I've been to Oregon only once, but they say you sometimes never forget the first time. I'm regularly haunted by idea that I'd be able to spend more time there. But enough of this nonsense; I can't paint such a picture if I haven't yet cast the stone into the river of blood.

Shall we get back to our dinner preparations? Rosa, Rosa, Rosa: When she cooks up a storm for one of the gatherings that occasionally take place for friends or former business associates, she does it all. Abi once decided that she'd bake two pies to contribute to our dinner; one was her cinnamon apple pie, the other a delightful lemon meringue, her father's recipe. And I made sure that Rosa picked up a plentiful supply of both strawberry and vanilla ice cream for little Elie.

Tonight on the menu there will be a variety of choices, and a few salads; I especially favored the Chinese chicken salad with blue cheese and teriyaki dressing, chopped spinach, and red cabbage. I rather enjoy Rosa's homemade lentil soup, and the purple yams marinating in butter, the roast beef, and coffee for desert—that's how my grandmother liked to do it, anyway. I find nostalgia is a nice place to visit.

It's 6:30 p.m., and the alley cats are on their sabbatical. I don't miss their wretched howls at sundown. Who takes their place but the loathsome boozers passing out down by the tire shop on the corner, leaving their cigarette butts nestled in with magnolia petals?

On the plus side of Los Angeles, though, is the Mediterranean climate. It's pleasant, even if at times it feels like a goddamn swamp, and the warming trend. . .well, it has made me suspicious about whether or not there'll be another functional decade ahead. I know this summer was going to far exceed triple digits. I guess you could say I was used to it.

Although the end of spring had made its way to my gate, echoing the call of the chaparral beyond the cityscapes, light winds swaying the palm trees lining Wilshire Boulevard. I like to keep the bay windows open on my balcony at this time of the day, filling my apartment with the evening breeze, the traffic, presumptuous and eight stories below, wailing like sirens from my youth. The buses ran less frequently as the day progressed, ushering in an opportunity for the promise of quiet, for once, to sleepwalkers and insomniacs.

And there it was again, the siren, louder now and then fading again—a reminder, a beacon.

Eleanor was sleeping on my couch, the most tender slumber. If only I could sleep that deeply. Not even if I had a half-dozen drinks the night before would I sleep half as well. I continued to putz around in the bathroom and around my bedroom, hanging up some clothing, and I cleaned the toilet. I looked well-rested in the bathroom mirror. I noticed a bit more white hair in my eyebrows, and on my arms as well, which I didn't exactly expect. My eyebrows were dark still, and I liked them framing my eyes. Abi once told me that I could get them professionally colored by a stylist and keep that youthful look. I was never much for those things, but I might consider some upkeep on those brows.

But enough of this already: I've got to wake Nora. She needs to use the restroom and get her shoes on before everyone else arrives. She was also a bit crabby before her nap, which makes me think she's been talking to her father again. I caught her at it last night, as I was tucking her in. She asked me if I wanted to ask her daddy a question about her mother. And I asked her what she meant, at first confused about how I should answer.

She elaborated for me: "Daddy can tell you anything about mother, if you want me to ask him. Like, do you want to know what her favorite flower is? 'Cause I forget."

If you must pry, I wasn't the slightest worried about her connection with John—she was young and still processing these things as best she could.

If Eleanor finds solace in thinking they're having a conversation, the truth is the world is full of misery. Why not color it in a little brighter? When I found her in the living room, she was hanging upside down, attempting to read my morning paper. She asked me if I often get paper cuts: such a smart question. I lifted her up into the air. Circling the dining room table and over by the bay windows I danced with her, almost knocking down the crystal vase from Abi, and my family heirloom --a wooden menorah painted with white daisies, atop the bookcase.

"So, my little lady, tell me how was your day in school? Did the teacher call on you, and did you know all of the answers?"

"No."

"I see," I said, fixing the hair on her braided ponytail and removing some sleep from her delicate eyes. She seemed quiet, more than usual. But I could always get her to open up a little more if necessary.

"And how is your math going? Did you start fractions?"

"Oh, yes, I'm good at fractions! Mom says I may become an engineer when I grow up and even fly airplanes. But I'm afraid to fly—it hurts my ears."

"It hurts your ears? Why so?"

"Well, every time we fly to Oregon to see Papa and Gramma Gigi, that's when they hurt me."

"So you don't like flying. Is that what you want to tell me?"

"Nope. I do not. Maybe they would move down here, so that I won't have to fly *all* the way there. They might like California. Yep. I think they might, they might. Don't you, sir?"

"Hm. I can't speak for your grandparents, but I *can* offer a solution."

"What's a soh-loo-shun?"

"You could say a solution is an answer to a question. Like when you do your fractions. The answer is the solution."

"So the plane is a math question? It's a number?"

"You could look at it that way, sure." I thought that was a reasonable answer—don't you?

"That's cool. A plane can be a number. A number can be a plane. A bird can be a rainbow. And a rock can be, can be... hm. Joseph, what can a rock be?"

"A rock can be an ice cream truck!"

"Oh, ice cream! *That's* what I need, oh yes I do. Please, sir, will you tell me when we can have some?" She played with my beard and tried to fit her eyeglasses on my face, and we laughed for what felt like forever and a moment longer. I decided I would ask my question and see how she responded. I'm still new to all of this, I keep telling myself. Just take it all in, breathe. It's been so long since I've felt this alive, not since I first saw Eden Ahbez in concert years back, when he was living in the Angeles National Forest. Topanga Canyon was just as wild as the stories you've heard. That was the last time I felt truly free and myself—until now, with Nora in my arms as if she has always been there. My old man once told me that I never had to be too desperate to impress others, that I had it in me naturally.

"Elie, can I ask you a question?"

"Well, Mother said I can't talk to strangers. But I talked to you, and now you're my friend, and Daddy says he likes you, so I think you can ask me a question, it's okay. I don't have to ask Mother. She knows who you are."

"Let me ask you this. . .what would you say if I drove us all up there, to Oregon, with your mom, so that your little ears won't have to hurt?"

"You *promise?"*

"Scout's honor!" I said with a salute. I set her down on the couch.

I'd been waiting for an excuse to head up the coast, to hit the open road way up beyond the city lights and following 1 North all the way into the Pacific Northwest, with views that would make one weep at such a sight, the trees of our ages seen by all of our ancestors, throwing our troubles on the dirt road. The endless coastal breeze.

Coincidentally, I'd been promising that trip to Abi—that in the early summer we'd get in the car and make it happen. I know she despises me right now, but the situation could be quite amusing. Maybe with age I can adapt to this new way of life, taking risks that I would otherwise argue against in my mind.

STEVE ARRIVED FIRST; HE CAME INTO THE HOUSE with Abi trailing behind him. He had a pie in each hand, with a big smile on his round (and now a bit chubbier) face. He had been putting on some weight recently. It's his desperateness for Samentha's love, and ever so recently he had admitted to me that he had been wondering if losing Kathy was a big mistake. I didn't put much effort into giving him advice on either matter, as I've learned recently that, when I extend myself in arenas that don't quite vibe with my own methodologies, I end up just getting myself into a whirlwind of emotions.

He was looking anxious almost immediately, though, as Sam hadn't yet arrived and it'd been over twenty-four hours since they had spoken or seen one another.

"Hey, Steve!" I asked. "You wanna hit the keys for our guests while I mix us some drinks?"

"Oh, of course. Yeah. . .I could do that. I mean if you don't think you need any help in the kitchen. . .um, do you know when Sam is getting here, by the way?" He waited, but I was much too busy playing with the girl with pink eyeglasses. I ran over to my piano and began to play a familiar song, one that Steve and I used to play together as a warm-up when we were still making music more on the fly: "Dancing Queen," by the infamous ABBA. Such a thrill, but I was still walking round in circles in my mind. Ever since Sam arrived, the truth is that things just haven't been the same. The sky, the walls of my apartment, they were continuously bathed in a whole other light that I wasn't used to. My eyes were still adjusting.

When I finished mixing everyone's drinks and came back out to the living room, I took to sitting with Abi for a bit on the patio. We had a few things to go over—mainly the fact that I had asked little Eleanor to talk to her mother about my driving them to Oregon. At first Abigail refused, but softly, as she's sometimes so good at. She had mentioned that it was important to her that I could follow through with my plan, that she wasn't going to label anything that was between us at this point. We had our separate lives; she took her travels seriously and wasn't willing to sacrifice those endeavors, and she wanted me to feel that I could pursue what was missing in my life. I was impressed and felt lighter in my skin. A blush came to her face, suddenly; the wine must have hit her. She took me into her arms and said that she'd changed her mind, that she would love to go on the trip, and that she wanted us to do it together—not as a couple, but as friends.

And if that was our closure for the next stage of our lives, that she was fine with that.

Closure. At the heart of this grand opening, the arrival of Sam and Nora, I had to make room for them in my life.

If you're wondering where Samentha could be, I was curious myself. It appears that she and Sandra were in the throes of a mighty potent conversation, one that I would have loved to be a fly on the wall for. But I can only tell you what she told me about why she never showed up for our dinner.

Sandra had met Samentha in the break room at the hospital, as she trailed off into a hush near the bulletin board, muttering the words, "I finally did it."

"You finally did what?" Sandra'd whispered back.

"I went to that place where they do the, uh, you know, the DNA testing."

Sam had leaned back against the soda machine, biting her nails and tightening her ponytail, taken out her Chapstick, and started to smell it too but hadn't put any on her lips.

"Ah. That place off of Gloria and Sunset?"

"Yep. I went in, and what's done is done. I gave them a sample of my blood. Felt as if I was coming into myself at that very moment. With each drop."

"I like what I'm hearing. You seemed so very timid when I first talked to you about it. But now, you're taking a chance. You feel good, no?"

"I think I do. Although this edginess in my stomach just won't go away." Sam had sat down then on one of the chairs beneath a few artificial hanging plants covered in dust and the relentless sorrows of every member of the hospital staff.

"That pain in your stomach, that may be there a while. And listen, the results could be disappointment, but either way, it's the next you. I like this." Sandra had reassured her that there was also more to all of it than just the results. It was about who she became during the process.

But of course, the results were the initial step, and all the strengths Sam would acquire would only bring her closer to me. She knew, as she had told me the Saturday before, that more than anything, the missing link to this whole strange scene was my presence.

"Well," she'd told Sandra, "I do have to say that, even if you thought I was nuts for going through with all of this, I'd still have done it. I didn't lose everything for no apparent reason. I know now that John's death was some sort of a sign."

"Yeah, the good lord often delivers his message with quite a sting when we need to see something we haven't been able to make sense of."

". . .Since when did we get so kinda spiritual?"

"I don't know, this year has been really so strange. Did we stumble into some sort of a portal? Anyway, what's it take, two weeks for the results, right?"

"That's what the paperwork says," Samentha had told her as she took a small folded envelope out of her bra, unfolded the document inside, and scanned it with tired eyes. Her hands had been trembling a bit, but with excitement.

"You're keeping it on your person. . .this is quite serious business." Sandra had begun to rub Sam's shoulders and adjust her wispy blonde bangs. "So you get tested, and then if there's a match, they let you know with a letter. Of course if your person of lineage is out there, they would have had to donate blood at some time or other."

"I don't care if they're dead, in prison, off on sabbatical on the other side of the country—just as long as I know who they are. So I can put the pieces together. Sandra. . . ."

"Yes?"

"I've felt this uneasy sort of emptiness for many, many years. I can be a whole person again now. At least for Nora."

"And for yourself—stop being so naive."

"You're right. I'm just a lonely feline howling away at the moon, waiting for some devoted tomcat to arrive. But I realize it's not just about sex or anything like that. Like, I'm attracted to Steve, but for some reason I can't get myself to look at him sexually. I need to solve this other puzzle. So that I can. . .find someone great, one day. Because even though I did love John, the truth is I still felt someone else was out there waiting for me."

"You weren't in love with your husband? Ever? Not even in the beginning?" Sandra asked, and Sam let out a great sigh, trembling the cement beneath her toes. Her nails were painted green.

"I just felt this need to have a child. And John seemed like a safe match. And he was stable, came from money. And he was *pretty*, that's for sure."

"The sex was good?"

"Once in a while, yeah."

"Come, let me put a Band-Aid on your little bleeding heart, if only for the next hour or so." Sandra reached out, and they embraced deeply for a moment. She offered to host her and Nora at her apartment for a Disney movie on the boob tube, but Samentha declined. It was roast beef night at Joseph's place, and she couldn't miss it for the world.

Sandra was not persuaded. "I say you leave the brat at home and we have a few extended hours together. I've got margarita mix. . .and an Edward Norton movie."

"Which one?" Sam felt the trench in her stomach start to settle. Maybe she just needed a break from everyone over there at the apartment, and the anxiousness never does subside.

"*Keeping the Faith*—it's from 2000. I've got it on DVD."

"A little Y2K temptation. Geez, I haven't even unpacked my DVD player. I think I left my one and only box of DVDs out in the sun on the patio the week we moved in. I just avoided getting them inside the house. I have yet to check out their condition."

"Oh, dear."

"Wait, isn't Ben Stiller in that, too?"

"Yep, and the score's by Bernstein. I know you like his work."

"This is true. Alright, lemme call Joseph. I'm sure he wouldn't mind spending a little extra time with Eleanor. Besides, I need to get a bit trashed. If you don't mind."

ON THE MORNING OF THE TRIP, I heard a knock on the door by a small hand once again, leaving no doubt of who it could be. Rise and shine, little one, mama's getting ready, your eyes are like the ocean, and I will bring the light back into your mother's.

Samentha was soon in the kitchen, pouring her coffee halfway. Then she sipped at it for a minute before adding cream. She was packing peanut butter and jelly sandwiches, some empty promises awaiting fulfillment, the leftover roast beef from the night of the great feast she never showed up to. But I forgave her, didn't make a big deal out of it. She'd been so cute when she showed up at my door around 3:00 a.m., her hair a mess, her sweater on backwards, and asked for the horoscope section of the paper, and whether Nora had been a good girl.

There we were, and we were devoting the second week in June to our trip, the second week of June. Really, it was no big deal for me to take a little time away from my routine; I've been retired long enough to expect that big plans are generally a piece of cake. Some may find that anything that feels like a challenge is problematic, and I acknowledge this fear, but then I let it go. Abi would argue that at times I dwell on it as well, which I also admit to.

Bend, Oregon, was on my radar. Senses abaft. With Abi along for the drive, and Steve staying behind—he'd been on bad behavior with Sam—the trip should be bittersweet and didn't need additional distractions.

The grandparents had been notified, Pops and Gigi awaiting our arrival. It would be quite something to meet John's parents. I was thinking about that quite a bit that morning, when I was relieving myself on my walk by the park past gruesome bench inhabitants, vomit and trash everywhere. Why add to the pleasantness?

Since the trip to Oregon is eight hundred miles long, I planned on getting there in just under three days—that is, if I could cover at least three hundred miles each day. We could stay in hotels for the first two nights, and by the third we should reach John's parents' house.

I left my small suitcase by the front door. I'm not one to take much with me on a trip, and I rather like to be an example for others who tend to overpack. But I don't like to preach this philosophy too much; it's better to lead with one's behavior than to be demanding. Sam was standing on the edge of the veranda, on the phone with the pharmacy. She wanted to pick up an antihistamine in case the ever-dreaded migraine made a sudden move during our trip. But she seemed to have light following her wherever she went. I took note of everyone's outfits: Sam in a green t-shirt, jeans, and light blue tennis shoes with small white daisies printed above heel. I had my Dodgers hat on, a white t-shirt, and a pair of jeans, too. I went with my white running shoes. I have a pair of black ones as well, three pairs of Tom's slip-ons, gifts from Abi over the past decade. She's always picked out just the right shoe for me—I can't explain it. I have a hard enough time finding a pair for myself. Nora wore red sandals, a salmon-colored cardigan, and blue shorts.

"Alright, crew, are we all ready to hit the open road?" I squealed over by the piano, playing us all a quick tune called "I'll Be Blue Just Thinking of You," by Aileen Stanley, originally recorded in August 1930, almost a hundred years back. Can you imagine? As the song came to a climax, Steve was saying his farewells to Samentha on his way downstairs. Sam had commented on the fact that he hadn't even offered to help us load up the car, and I do believe that, when a woman makes up her mind about something, she'll generally stick to her guns unless persuaded otherwise. But that process often takes months, even years. I was daydreaming about the massive moss-covered tree trunks we were all about to embark on, and that humble air that was to grace my lungs for once.

I turned the car around toward Sunset Boulevard and veered left towards the 405. It was time to pick up Abi.

I imagined her waiting out by the round-about, beneath the bougainvillea, with her small white suitcase, large white sun hat, and her auburn slacks. After we picked her up (god-willing she was in a good enough mood), we could start curating the music for the road. I had packed two cases of CDs filled with albums by The Bay City Rollers, Petr Pavel, Barry Walker Jr., Vig Mihaly, Yukjii Asaoka, Elton John, The Everly Brothers, The Funkees, and many others. I had taken the time to alphabetize each album, so that, if someone had a request, all they'd have to do is sort through the alphabet.

I reached the 110 in a matter of minutes and would take the 1 North all the way into Oregon. It would be Abi's first visit to the Pacific Northwest.

She puttered around in the ice chest that we had settled into the back of the trunk. Showtunes was the first request, then we moved on to a few Disney songs. But soon, after a few of those rather obnoxious tunes, I asked for some Gershwin, and afterwards a little Hadda Brooks. The slow and elusive morning turned into noon, and being it was early June, there was a corporeal gloom of fog and haze. This mortal coil of time and the essence of the distance required one to reach a place beyond fear . . .Sam would embody this feeling—almost like the light azure glaze of the ocean, right as we passed San Luis Obispo. Eleanor was counting how many birds she saw on the trees; she was already up to 112. But by that point, her mother was getting ready to check-out.

That's when something miraculous occurred: Abi invited the child to join her in a different game—"a silent sort of tango" is how she described it to her. "Like the snail," she said. "Be steady and aware of the trail you leave behind you."

They would begin by drawing pictures of something in the car, then finding something outside the windows, out on the road, that would be fun to imagine adding to the drawing. Abi continued, "Let's say that I'm going to draw this shoe here. See? It's white, and it has laces and a few holes for the laces to fit into. Then, as we drive along. we can spot something on the road that might be a similar match with the shoes."

"What does *that* mean?"

"That's a great question! So right now, if we look out our window, we can spot tractors, right? And there are a few cows, and there up ahead we can see a small house painted white—out there in the distance, you see that?"

"I do, I do!"

"So I will choose to draw this white house right next to these white sneakers, and that's how we make a *correlation*."

"A cora-mason?"

"Exactly. But we'll talk more about that later. For now, just look for something that reminds you of the white shoes. I chose the white house over there. You can choose. . .hmmm." She stopped and looked around more.

But before she could utter a word, Eleanor jumped into her lap and screamed, "I can draw that *white bird!* And then. . .and then we can put on our shoes and take the white bird into the white house!"

"You're quite bright, aren't you, little one?" Abi gathered her thoughts, took a deep breath, and looked at me in the rear view mirror, smiling in a way that I hadn't seen since our first kiss. I thought her game was brilliant, actually. I could never have come up with something so elaborate, and I could tell that Samentha was moved by the effort.

Three hours passed, and I was aiming to make it to Carmel for our two rooms by the sea: Abi and I in one room, Sam and Eleanor in the other. The sun began to descend behind the ocean; it was 4:00 p.m., and we had been cruising at seventy-five miles an hour with barely any effort, as the six cylinders carried the all the heavy lifting. Toward the end of the drive, we discovered an enchanting radio station that allowed us all to dive deep into the well of much of the music I had grown up with: Townes Van Zandt, Jelly Roll Morton, Paul Simon, Jerry and the Catalinas . . .another endless list.

Sam was relieved to finally have some time away from the hospital, and for most of this first leg of the trip she had confessed, multiple times, to feeling ready to quit her job. She had noted that, in many ways, her leaving Oregon was when she initially felt the urge to change professions. But she had to stick to her plans to support her daughter; there wasn't any room for excuses then. You have to make sacrifices for your children, but what I've come to learn is that for some reason we got it wrong all these years. It's not that you have to sacrifice anything, it's more a collaboration with another person or situation.

Eleanor never did very well sleeping in a strange house, so I had been told. We might be stuck on the road with a little monster, so to speak, which I was fully prepared to take on—it was my pleasure. But she'd been encouraged to sleep during the car ride, so aside from the bird-counting dilemma and the white shoes game, Nora had been a pretty drowsy participant during the trip so far.

We reached The Dolphin, a hotel with an attentive staff dressed in red jackets and hurrying towards us, handling our bags, and rambling on about how it was their prerogative to meet our demands as their guests. Samentha woke Nora and carried her sleepy body from the car. The rest of us were somewhat exhausted from the drive, hungry, and eager for the next two days to pass just as smoothly as today. We entered the lavishly decorated lobby, where a gold-chained chandelier hung from the brightly lit ceiling. The chairs, arranged in a half-circle by the lobby, were calling to me. I just had to stretch out but couldn't imagine wandering around or standing up for much longer than a few minutes. I wondered how I would feel by day three, not having access to my piano or my bay windows. Would Steve take good care of my place while I was gone, or is this when he loses his shit? Kathy has been on his mind lately. Samentha still hadn't put-out, and since he'd been putting on that extra weight (which he generally is very self-conscious about), I thought his self-confidence was dwindling. This may be his mid-life crisis, having arrived a little earlier than most people's. I made sure that Nora's had access to the washroom downstairs, since I knew there'd be moments when she would wander and need to use the restroom.

I checked us all in at the front desk while everyone else took a look around the ground floor of the hotel. Near the stairwell sat a small aquarium housing the Pearl gourami, cyprinids and catfish, Neon tetras and Harlequin rasboras, not excluding the Cherry barb and the Siamese algae eater.

I was informed that there was a restaurant close by. Some drinks could be had. The light pink building housed about fifty rooms and was only two stories, we'd come to discover—no basement, no attic. The familiar aroma of the lobby brought me back to the late Sixties, when I was traveling around more in each country.

That perfumed lobby never did escape me. If I avoid any mirrors I can, at once, feel like my younger self, as if I've gone back in time and my body feels as it did then. And my eyes aren't as heavy upon waking. And I still have a chance to find someone to start a family with, this symbolic moment between myself, Samentha, Nora. . .and perhaps Abi is a part of it now as well. I can't be sure. Sometimes her intentions are thoughtful but I am curious if she will follow through connecting with my little Eleanor.

CHAPTER EIGHT

BEND, POPULATION 100,000

AS THE SUN COLLAPSED BEHIND THE OCEAN, we decided to turn in early for the night. We'd have plenty of sightseeing to do over the course of the next few days. I helped Samantha repack a few things that were out of order from the car ride. Abi was surprisingly more upbeat than usual and looking forward to a little time to herself in our hotel room.

I stayed with Sam for a bit to help her get settled in to her own room. We talked very little about Oregon and instead focused mainly on what places would be suitable for Nora to explore. The only place I wanted to take everyone was in a tiny refuge in San Francisco, close to the town of Pacifica, called Lake Merced—an unassuming sanctuary that housed various bird species native to the Bay. I'd only been there once, decades before, but it had always haunted me when I thought about my thirties.

Samantha laid Eleanor into the queen size bed and covered her, first, with her baby blanket, the one item that goes wherever she does; she had me help her with the comforter a bright green knit piece on the ottoman, which I found a bit hideous. I helped Sam lock up and checked all the outlets to make sure nothing would catch fire in the middle of the night.

"I'll probably get a bath," she said, then hit the hay. It's a little early for me, but my mind will be wandering for another few hours. I'll eventually get to sleep, though."

"Alright, then, just let Abi and me know if there's anything you two need. I'm gonna head downstairs for a drink, Abi's got a game of chess going, so we'll be up a bit longer."

While soaking in the warm water, eradicating any rancid thoughts, the suds put Sam's mind at ease for the first time in weeks. She thought about Steve. How they'd started to be more intimate lately. . .six months since the first time they had met at my apartment on the day she moved into the complex. It feels so long ago, but if I'm to be real about the whole thing, everything escalated kind of fast among the five of us. Sam had started to develop more feelings for Steve, but the truth was that she wasn't attached. It was almost as if she was waiting to feel something more. I mean, sure, she felt something. . . but it wasn't the real thing. The two had spent the night together the previous week, when Eleanor was staying over at a classmate's apartment. This helped Sam feel a bit less inhibited when she allowed him to look into her eyes, to speak sweetly, to touch her. She had refused him less and less, but there still wasn't an emotional attachment, she had confessed to me earlier in the morning. She had sensed that Steve felt the gap between them, but they both remained silent about it, as if neither wanted to talk about it again, especially after that one tragic night at the movie theatre. Steve wanted to forget that whole embarrassing predicament.

And they had yet another argument a few weeks before their one sensual engagement. But through some good hard growth (from my own tepid standpoint), it seemed to me that he was finally able to understand her slightly better. He wasn't sulking as much as he had; on the contrary, he'd begun to feel closer to her. Before we left on our trip, I noticed he was growing more patient and even, dare I say, respectful toward her and her situation. He had finally grasped what made her tick—that she meant what she said, said what she meant, with no hidden agenda. She wasn't like most women her age. And she wasn't such a complicated person after all, Steve had discovered. In the nature of his work, though, every person he encountered *had* that hidden agenda he so feared in the intimate realm. This expectation was engrained in that wet little brain of his. And this rusty and snippy attitude had carried over into his personal life. It's unfortunate but to be expected. I forgave Steve anyway, but Sam was still far too distant for his liking.

Either way, it was time I stopped ruminating on the situation. I had a light Pilsner at the bar and did some writing. I'd been feeling indifferent about further collaborations with Steve, especially on the level of us making music again. But even so, I had done a bit of composing in my head earlier that day and wanted to be sure I had jotted some of the parts down before they left me. I wouldn't forget the melody itself—it'd be running through my mind until I can sit at the piano again.

I had been listening to a lot of Alan Planes right before the trip, especially "Impromptus D. Thema Andante." It was something I imagined one day playing for Nora. So I guess you could say that piece was an inspiration for what I'd clumsily scribbled down. I keep a folded-up piece of paper in my pocket at all times on which I write out ideas for new songs. At the end of each week, I put sheet into a folder with all the others, and I then sit down with all these ideas on the very last day of the month, stitching the pieces together. "Thema Andante" was a song originally composed by Robert Schumann, for the *Etudes Symphoniques Opus 13*. I came to fancy this song, particularly for its variations. "Andante" is an Italian word that translates to "at a moderate pace," which I rather liked to think about. Moving along with such a playful tempo, as it slides down through my stubborn subconscious, allows me to drift along as I may, without explanation, without analyzing any numbers or any of those wretched things.

At 11:00, I made my way back upstairs. The hall to our floor was flushed with too bright a light, almost nauseating, especially at that hour. I had worn the most uncomfortable pair of shoes on the trip. Why I had not packed an extra pair of running shoes, I couldn't tell you. Perhaps it was Abi's bitching that made me rush into packing, leaving out various things that I would have normally doubled up on.

As I made my way to the door where we were staying, I instead imagined Samentha in her own hotel room, perhaps still awake, looking around at her surroundings, alone, quietly mourning the process of her life, taking a deep breath, pouring a cup of water from the bathroom faucet, and shaking off her socks at the side of the bed. I pictured her lying back slowly and finally closing her eyes, anticipating the meeting with her in-laws, forging her own silence, reflecting on nothing but the sound of her daughter's breathing.

But enough dreaming already: I entered the room and called out for Abi. She was in the bedroom already, no robe or pajamas, just a t-shirt and some sweatpants. Recently she'd taken up smoking, which was something I never judged her for, as she never smoked more than a few cigarettes a month. It was a habit she given up just before I met her, all those years back. But around the fall of the previous year she'd started up again on one of her trips to Greece. And as she began to peel back the covers, I could smell the faint aroma of tobacco as I moved closer to her in the bed.

"I like Eleanor," she began, and I was a bit taken back for a moment. But I was also slightly drunk. The bed had obscenely large pillows, uncomfortable and too soft. Who wants to be swallowed in such an abyss? I've always preferred one type of pillow, flat and thin. I like to lie back as if I were out in a field in the moonlight. When I was a boy, my father would take me out to the plains, and we'd camp there for a night or two when my mother was going stir-crazy in the house, and it was clear she needed a little break.

As did my father. The two of them got along for the most part, and I recall them being quite affectionate with one another both at home and in public. But as I got older, especially around age eleven, I became more aware of my own mortality. And theirs.

Nora would soon reach the age where her mind would begin to wonder more about all the little things she'd never noticed when she was, say, six or seven.

There I go again, getting distracted. I hadn't answered Abi, almost didn't feel like getting into it. But I did. "So you like her, do you? Warming up to her charm? Took you long enough."

"Yeah, I do. But she does get on my nerves now and then, especially when she carries on about some stupid song. I mean, really. . .I never listened to cartoon songs when I was her age. I think my first album was Brahms."

"Well," I said as I took off my shirt and adjusted my watch, "the thing is, not everyone's had the opportunity to listen to Brahms as a child. You're a rare bird."

"I dunno. She could have better taste in music, and that's Sam's job, to provide her with some more-intellectual influences. I mean, the way that kid carries on in the car and opens the window when it's just much too cold outside—I really feel Samentha could be a better disciplinarian, too."

Abi sat up in bed a bit more and put on her green cardigan--the one she always slept in, even it was a warm summer night.

"She's only eight years old, Abi, still so—so very young. I gotta say, there are a ton of things she has yet to discover about the world, and how she fits into it." For someone as advanced and tenacious as Abi (in her best moments), her comment embarrassed me. How could she be so naive?

"Well," she went on, "my mother was strict, and it made me who I am. I don't take any bullshit, not to mention my dad being short-tempered. That was a lot to deal with."

"This isn't about you," I said.

"Excuse me? I'm in this just as much as you are. So if I choose to make a connection, correlation, whatever you want to call it—this absurd situation—just let me be me. Is that too much to ask?"

"That's just it."

"What?"

"Samentha is a patient person. She allows for the child to be a child. I don't notice any irregular behavior."

"Oh, so you know everything, do you? Look at you, like some sort of a desperate guru, latching on to that poor woman and her kid. This is just all too funny, coming from you, Jack. All of a sudden, you've got all of this experience about being a parent."

"Give me the benefit of the doubt here. When my parents were patient with me, it taught me to carry that same behavior into my adult life. When I got out of line, the house rules weren't so rigid. My mother's attitude toward me was actually similar to how Samentha handles Elie. There's room for discomfort that the child causes her, on occasion, but. . . ."

"I'm not following you."

"Oh, good lord, Abi."

"Educate me."

". . .The thing is, I remember so many of my friends whose parents would put them in their place, right in front of whoever was around. But humiliation isn't healthy for a child. It causes problems later on. Rigid house rules are not so much a measure of discipline but a convenience for parents, to avoid the painful process, the discomfort, that the children inflict on them. You see, Abi, I just. . .we've talked about this before. I don't know why you act so surprised every time."

"Uh-huh."

"There's a very fine line between enforcing rules for discipline and proper child development."

"I see that. I do. I mean, my upbringing stifled my development, sure, if that's what you want me to admit. Of course it did. But it gave me a little hair on my chest."

"Don't try and charm me. This is serious."

"You're drunk."

"Either way, it's essential that I tell you these things. I don't care if you take them to heart, it doesn't matter."

"Oh, Jack, you're such a cad." She stared at the ceiling, ruffled her hair a bit, and scooted farther away from me.

"I once saw a good friend of mine," I said, "who was raising her daughter as a single mom after a long, drawn out divorce. . .messy, just awful. The kind you overhear someone talking about at a diner, you know? The husband was an absolute schmuck, never around yet demanded that his needs be met. He worked very little, and whenever he *was* around her and their daughter, he showed very little interest, I'll tell you that."

"Maybe she wasn't very interesting."

"She was a good seed."

"Yeah, you probably had a thing for her, too."

"Anyway, there was one night when her daughter wouldn't stop crying. And this mother, a friend of the family, *not* my love interest, mind you. . .she'd been taught to just let the child cry it out, and if they didn't stop, you sent them to bed without supper or a bath, isolated in their bedroom, as a punishment. The child complied, but not without indignation."

"Yeah, so?"

"Abi, I felt strongly that what that girl really needed was a few extra minutes with her mom—to be read another story, to be carried upstairs and get a bath, put into her pajamas, and wait to be tucked in. But my friend took the easy way out instead, asserting her authority, because she could. Because she just wanted—needed even—some peace and quiet.

If only she'd approached her daughter in a different way. . .but she didn't want to part with her frustration with the child."

"Are we done here? I'm absolutely about ready to pass out."

"I don't know, Abi, this feels so one-sided. I might as well be talking to a brick wall. It's like this: People shouldn't take on parenting before the age of thirty."

"Oh, *that's* your main argument. It's weak."

"Samentha runs the extra mile, even after an intense day at the hospital. She'll be exhausted, and it won't faze her, prevent her from caring for child. It sends a message that, *as* a child, she has certain rights. And in turn she'll grow into herself gracefully, develop self-worth and resilience. Children are disruptive, they kick and scream, and eventually they grow out of it. Of course there are destructive levels of behavior that could be a whole other issue. Some children are really uncontrollable—but this isn't the case with Eli or my friend's daughter. To be a parent is to know courage, and to understand the sacrifices you need to make."

I looked at Abi and realized that she was already asleep, her breathing slow and soft, as if somehow made innocent again. And her breasts, small and firm, rose and fell, and I laughed for a second to myself.

Maybe I liked the chaos that Abi caused in me. All that lecturing for nothing. Nothing but a glance into my strange muse's slumber. I turned and switched off the lamp on the nightstand, leaned over her slightly, shut my eyes, and drifted off to sleep.

AT 6:42 A.M., NORA AWOKE LATE, after Abi and I had gotten ready. Samentha was still in bed. I entered their room to check on their status. Eleanor looked around at the unfamiliar items on the nightstand. A pensive and sauntering current from the open window veiled her eyes. They swam around visions of soon-to-be ocean waves at her toes. Memories of her father had begun to fade (recently, I'd seen it in her eyes). But he still makes an appearance, her steady ghost who slowly dissipates into each and every morning. She sees me standing in the doorway of their bedroom but says nothing, adjusts her hairband, takes it off and chews on it for a minute.

I can tell she feels secure lying next to her mother, cuddling, with her legs hanging over the side of the bed. I wondered if she was hungry, so I motioned for her to follow me out to the kitchenette. We tiptoed out together.

I offered Nora a banana, but she made a disgusted face and started to laugh at my shirt, which I had no idea was inside out. If only she knew how lovely she was, and that she deserved to have a father in her life, sotmeone who would notice these little things about her development.

I was surprised that she didn't even want to try the croissants I had picked up earlier—they were still warm. She wanted something else, but she didn't know what. I ran through the variety of snacks we had in the fridge. She didn't want something cold, and she didn't want anything that had to be cooked. So I pulled out the only other option—a box of cereal, and not the most exciting type for someone so young. But Nora reached into the box of corn flakes and began to chomp on a handful ever so delicately.

"Mommy likes to sleep sometimes, she really does."

"She needs the extra z's, dear—it's good we didn't wake her. Do you want some milk, or are you just snacking there?"

"Maybe I want some milk, but for later. I wanted to ask you if me and daddy can eat on the balcony so we can look at the ocean together."

"I don't see why not! Come, I'll bring us a bowl and we can pour some in here. . .there we go, see? It's better in a bowl, don't you think?"

"Sure! I like this bowl," she said in a whisper, looking beneath it and inside, holding it above her as if it were suddenly a sacred object.

"And why's that?" I asked.

"Because."

"Any reason why?"

"I think I like it. . .'cause *you* like it," she whispered again, hid her face behind the bowl, and said nothing further.

"Oh, aren't you the clever one!"

"Clevh-err? You mean I'm a clover?"

"Not exactly. . .see, a clover is a small plant."

"Can I eat clover?"

"Hm. I'm not sure about that one. But, 'clever' means, well, it means that you're very smart, and it surprises me sometimes."

"I surprise you, like it's your birthday?"

I picked Eleanor up and carried her out onto the balcony. "You surprise me because I don't meet many girls who are so very smart, like you."

"Oh, I think I understand." I ran my hands through her hair and poked her little nose twice, and she in turn threw a handful of corn flakes in my direction. We laughed and made a mess on the patio. It was one of the best moments in my life.

We watched the ocean and all its majesty spread its luminescence across the white foam, rushing to the shore with each transparent wave. I imagined a fire burning on the water, as if god had set the ocean aflame to remind me that this was real. Apprehensive seagulls danced on skinny legs in the white sand, and I imagine the ions in the water's source entering her small lungs.

A screech broke the silence from the other side of the dunes, and a large green truck came into view and began to empty garbage bins. Nora ran from her seat to close the sliding doors, but Samentha had already been awakened by the roar of the engine that started and stopped. It was 7:13 a.m.

WE WERE ALL SEATED IN THE DINING ROOM after returning from a trip to the long buffet table, covered in a white cloth, on which lay plates of hors d'oeuvres and round silver dishes filled with scrambled eggs on hot plates, a platter with link sausages, and a small white basket filled with bagels and pumpkin rolls. Next to a dish with little butter cubes sat pastries of all shapes and aromas, and an enormous coffee urn that called my name.

Hotel guests were spilling in from the outside world as if nothing existed of someone else's life past those revolving doors. Some came with disheveled hair and half-awake mutterings about their drowsy morning, which spilled over the empty space between my heart and the next few days of our journey: rise-and- shine assholes. A few small children were sitting beside their parents, but I couldn't see their faces. Everything felt a bit blurry suddenly, and I wondered if it was because I was growing more nervous as each minute overshadowed the last.

"So, kids, we could get to San Francisco in about three hours, possibly even less than that if we leave soon enough to miss the rush right around eleven," Abi said; she always gets a bit impatient in the morning.

"Oo! We can take Eleanor to the Wharf. Maybe take a short boat trip to Alcatraz?" I suggested, with a mouthful of watered- down coffee.

"Should we spend the night there?" Abi asked.

"Yeah, why not? We can go check out Oakland, too. There are some nice museums on that side of the Bay. Hands-on type places."

"Yes, Mama, I wanna go everywhere you go. And where Joseph goes, too."

"Oh, of course. Of course, my little sweet pea. We'll paint the city pink!" Samentha cried out with a smile so pure that I choked on my own saliva, overcome by a serenity I'd never felt before. And I took a deep breath.

"We can paint the city?"

"Oh, my god, can we get on the road now?" Abi snapped.

I could only hope that she put a muzzle on for the second act. Day two on the road, and I'm honestly feeling like I should have listened to my intuition and let her stay behind. "Did you know, Eli, that, on Fisherman's Wharf, you can see how they make chocolate?"

I continued to describe all the marvelous sights in San Francisco. While doing so, I motioned for the others to grab their bags so we could pack up the car. I was still feeling a bit dizzy but I didn't mention anything to the others. An odd thing happened when I picked up Eleanor, though—she turned to me and placed a palm on my forehead. I saw her do it as if in slow motion, her skin like porcelain against my own wretched complexion.

"Jo, you should know that Daddy thinks you're going to be alright. He says don't worry."

"Oh, I, uh, that's very nice of him to say," I told her, tearing up quickly, holding back a heavy sob I felt coming on deep in my stomach.

"Alright, guys," Samentha said a few minutes later, "I just got off the phone with Martha and Dean. They're anxiously awaiting our arrival. Even the neighbors are tickled. This is gonna be a blast. I wanted to make sure that I thank you all for coming along on this trip."

I zoned out, trying my best to hold in my tears a little longer. *Don't be a goddamn fool,* I was telling myself. *You can handle this.*

"Oh, Sam," Abi said, "we wouldn't be here if we didn't want to be. It's an honor." I was taken back again by her performance. If only she'd say such nice things to me when we had our talks.

"That's really kind of you to say, Abi. I've never taken on this type of an endeavor, so I'm a bit out of sorts here and there."

"Well, I'm a bit *ferklempt* myself, as I am used to flying. Driving just takes much too long. But yeah, I'm happy to be here. For the journey. Thanks for having me aboard, Sam. I know I can be a bit hot-headed at times."

We all laughed. Samentha smiled that deeply haunting smile I just adore, and I looked out toward the revolving doors again, watching bits of sun break through the fog. The one thing I absolutely favor about the Bay area is that there are no mosquitos. Those things get on my nerves down south. I wondered if it was a certain blood-type they were attracted to.

By a quarter to twelve, Abi fell asleep in the car for the ride down to the Wharf, but first we parked down in Chinatown. There was a nostalgic spot where Sam said she and John frequented on their annual visits, and I was already starving for a window seat, ramen, and steamed vegetables. It was a vegetarian Chinese restaurant, and by noon the usual rush from the locals filled our eyes with wonder.

When we reached the Ghirardelli Chocolate Factory, we let Eleanor take lead on how she wanted to navigate the experience. Her elbows were covered in milk chocolate, and her chin had raspberry remnants that bugged the hell out of Abi, but Sam and I didn't bother to clean her up yet.

"I've come to the conclusion that I'm allergic to children, but just remember, my dear. . .I'm doing this for *you*." whispered Abi while Sam and Nora were galivanting around the white chocolate-covered prunes display. There were roses out front of the shop, and I thought about picking one or two for the car ride.

But before I did anything silly and obvious, we made our way to the Island of Alcatraz. Tickets were, relatively, a blow to the pocketbook, around a hundred bucks each for the tour.

Since we hadn't made our way to Lake Merced, I really wanted to take us up to Muir Woods, another place I always passed by when roving in the skies above the primeval redwoods. But such venerable landmarks often get missed when traveling with more than one person. I'd thought about how nice it would have been if it was just Eli and Sam by my side. I didn't dare mutter anything of the sort to Abi.

Dinner was served back at the hotel dining room from 7:00 to 9:00 p.m. I was craving a pastrami on rye; Sam mentioned a Waldorf salad. Abi was hankering for coleslaw, but a *horiatiki salata* would suffice. Eleanor wanted a bowl of cereal, but Samentha wasn't so keen on the idea. Eli ran up to me, grabbed onto my legs, and begged me for a bowl of cereal in her favorite bowl. I promised her that, when we returned to our rooms, she could have a small bowl, but that, for now, it was important that we all had the right sort of nourishment. "Snacking can come anytime," I said. "Just you wait."

"I'm always *waiiiting!* Waiting for the sun to come up. Waiting for Daddy. Waiting for school to end. Waiting for Mommy to make a decision." Nora babbled on and on as Abi suddenly got up to use the restroom.

"Honey, what's this about me making a decision? What decision?" Sam asked the child, with quite a worried rush under her breath.

"Daddy told me that you have to make a decision. I don't want to explain it—he doesn't want me to give away the secret."

"What *secret,* sweet pea? What are you talking about? See, Joseph, this is what I was saying all along— it's not good for her to have these strange thoughts." Samentha started fussing with Eli's hair, and I watched as a blush came to her face. She swallowed hard a few times, tearing up a bit.

"I think it's innocent, Sam. Let's just go along with it a little longer. When we get back to L.A., we'll talk about some t-h-e-r-a-p-y. Alright?" I assured her that the time would come for us to further investigate what to do about Nora's ghost-talk. But for now, we'd finish up our dinner.

Samentha put Eleanor to bed shortly after we finished our wine, and joined me and Abi downstairs for a nightcap. I could hear the Muni passing by as it stopped up the block to allow the nightcrawlers to board. I may have had a bit too much coleslaw, since Abi ordered such a large portion and I just can't resist sometimes. Sam came back at our space at the bar with our drinks and started the conversation by thanking Abi for sticking around and putting up with an eight-year-old on the road. "I imagine at times, if you don't mind me observing, that she gets on your nerves a bit."

"There were a few moments when I thought I was gonna lose it, I have to say. But she's just the cutest thing. . .and *that*, coming from me of all people, says a lot. She's a good kid, Sam."

"Thank you. Really. I, um, it's been an adjustment for the two of us. Away from her grandparents especially worries me. They were the ones who practically raised her, after John was gone." Sam took a gulp of her bloody mary like a rebel.

"I have to confess, until I met Eleanor, I didn't know much about children. I don't have nephews or nieces. It's just not my thing. I don't get kids. My brothers were all older than me, so I can't remember much about what it was like to be around someone younger. . .so I never knew much about the patience necessary for such encounters. Joseph has given me some good advice though, quite recently," Abi added, surprising me.

"Oh, is that so? Joseph does get along great with my daughter. It means a lot to me. She really does need someone in her life, a father figure. I hope you don't mind sharing him with her," Sam giggled and nudged me.

"Well," I said, "we've got another five hours to go tomorrow, so I'm gonna turn in my towel, let the night envelop me, as they say. You ladies have a nice night."

"Oh—well, I'll come to bed too, honey," said Abi. "I don't need to talk Sam's ears off."

"It's totally fine, I enjoy the conversation. And the company! Stay, we'll have one more drink. No?"

"Alright. I guess we can let the old man get to bed before he gets all crabby."

"Okay you two," I said, "enjoy yourselves. Don't talk about me too much while I'm gone."

"Night, Jack."

"Goodnight. . .Jack? Wait, why do you call him Jack? Have I been calling you the wrong name all this time?" Sam asked, startled and embarrassed, looking toward me, but I was already on my way toward the stairwell, listening to their voices and laughter droning over the hum of the vending machines and night scum out on the patio sucking down another cigarette before their next whiskey on the rocks.

As soon as I got upstairs I fell into a deep sleep. But to my surprise, I awoke to Abi spooning me from behind, stroking my hair as I fell in and out of a dream, replaying the day out in my mind, thinking about Sam and Eleanor. For a moment I wondered about Steve, but for some reason I got the feeling that he would be alright. Even if Sam decided she wanted to move back to Oregon, it didn't matter much to me either way. I'd savor this trip.

By morning, the sun was fighting hard to break through the heavy fog and began to flicker on the Golden Gate Bridge, a reflected scintillation off in the distance from the hotel balcony. The California–Oregon border was behind us now, and now the laurel figs, Monterey cypresses, and other riparian shrubs were replaced by the black cottonwood, the Western hemlock, and even ponderosa pine. It was as if we were being swallowed by the forest surrounding us on the highway, haunted by such splendor, a dominion that far surpasses the static crumminess of Los Angeles.

The sun was moving west, making the drive a little easier on our eyes. As we passed through the Southern Oregon Siskiyous we were cocooned by the swath of roadside flower beds—the harvest brodiaea, Aquilegia Formosa, and some evening primrose. Eleanor was shouting each and every time she spotted a deer at the edge of the forest. And then came the counting game, however many birds she spotted atop the trees that she accounted for.

I liked this game myself, quite a bit. We were already up to 112 birds. But by then, her mother was getting ready to check out. I didn't blame her.

TWO HOURS LATER, CRATER LAKE WAS ON OUR LEFT, so we parked and stretched by the sunny cascades, listening carefully to the sound of nothing. Nora was eagerly awaiting the arthropods—a new word she had learned in school and kept repeating throughout our trip. I myself was more interested in the Ceanothus silk moth, and the Zephry anglewing butterfly. I would look for them, streamside, and tell Nora about their egg-laying abilities.

"See, these ones here tend to be attracted to the amino acids in tree sap. But occasionally they will become a bit ill from feasting on too much rotting fruit. . .also one of their favorite things to eat."

"Rotting fruit? That's so gross, Jo!"

"Indeed it is, but just as we enjoy a burger, or some ice cream—"

"Ice cream! Give it to me! You have some?"

"No, no. I was just making a comparison."

"Comparisssun?"

"Indeed. The butterfly, in this case, has a taste for rotting fruit. Something you and me would find disgusting."

"Yuck!" she said, grinning with excitement.

"Exactly. But, the butterfly would most likely find ice cream disgusting."

"Is that true? How could anyone ever think that ice cream is bad? I don't know if I like these butterflies. They're kind of stupid."

"Well, now, you can't call someone a name like that just because they're different."

"Okay. I'm sorry. I'm sorry, butterflies!"

"It's alright. I tell you what—after our hike, we'll go back to our lodging, over by the woods and the red barns, and we will make a drawing of a butterfly who likes to eat ice cream."

"Oh, yes. Oh, that would be my pleasure!" The women rolled their eyes at me, and we continued on our hike through the dramatic rabbitbrush, as we navigated past glimpses of nettle and the hibernating nectar of the birch trees. Abi and I would spend some more time here the next day, and camp out together alongside the cabins. Although I was looking forward to that night, I also got this feeling of disenchantment. I wanted to lay instead under the stars with Sam and little Eleanor, deploying my senses beneath the guise of a different life, a future that I could taste, one that I knew was on its way. Each day was a different phase. Regardless of these meandering follies, we would leave Crater Lake and arrive at the grand terminus: Bend, Oregon—population 100,000.

CHAPTER NINE

THE WILKINSONS'

THE MAIL BOX ON THE FRONT GREEN LAWN carried the legend *Welcome to the Wilkinsons' Home.* Martha heard the car first, as her husband's hearing was almost gone, and he refused to use a hearing aid. "Only old people wear those contraptions," Dean would mutter.

She came running out of the small house, and Eleanor jumped onto her, almost knocking her onto the grass. Martha was surprised by how much the child had grown since she last saw her. It made her feel older. She threw an arm around her daughter-in-law and came over to greet Abi and me.

"Please, do come in. Dean's waiting inside—he's on the phone as usual." She helped us grab some of our luggage, playing with Eleanor's hair and asking her so many questions that the little girl felt an excitement she'd truly missed.

Martha and Dean's home had been built in 1964. There was some remodeling that could be done, as Dean often got a bit pushy about, but Martha liked all the tiny nuances of their home and wouldn't change a thing.

Well, there was one thing she would: She wished that Dean would find the time to look at the little things that made her excited about life. She'd always wanted to build an aviary in the front yard, so that when families passed their house they could learn something new about birdlife. She imagined painting small signs with names and a portrait of the different feathered friends that inhabited the aviary. Dean was only interested in his area of the house: his bedroom, his phone calls, his own thing. I guess you could call his behavior masculine, but I often find hard to relate to that nonsense.

"He'd often eat all the food in the fridge," Sam told me, "leaving very little for his wife to count on when she wanted a snack—or a glass of orange juice, for Chrissake."

"Well, I'm guessing that John was more like his mom. . .or at least, I'm hoping."

"No, John was a good guy. His father is really a complete terror though."

"I appreciate you giving me the scoop."

"Alright, let's get the rest of our things. Is Abi inside already?"

"I imagine she might be."

"She doesn't really wait for you or help you with things like this?"

"Well, I haven't really traveled with her very often, to tell you the truth. It's. . .well it's kind of—"

"Embarrassing?"

"That would be the case. I can vouch for it. But I'm so used to it."

"You deserve better," she said flatly. "But to be continued. He gets anxious, and Martha will need a little extra attention while we're here."

"I'm here, Samantha. Okay? I'm here. You see me, don't you?"

"I do. I see you. Just watch out what you say to him. He's going to try his best to dominate the conversation, and he's not afraid to put anyone in their place. Not that anyone belongs to wherever he assigns any of us."

Sam was beginning to seem overwhelmed, and I didn't blame her. "Let's do this," I said, reaching to grab her suitcase.

"THE LIVING ROOM IS SO SPACIOUS, and the ceiling is. . .what would you call that?" I asked Martha.

"Vaulted. That was the one thing that caught our attention when we first bought the house—didn't we, Dean? . . . Dean?" Martha trailed off. He was standing by the front door, looking at our car.

"Dean, honey, don't you like the ceilings? They were asking you?"

"Yeah, yeah, the ceilings are. . .ahh, I never cared much for this place. I'd rather it be a little on the smaller side. I don't have time to be wandering around the house making sure things are in order. That's Martha's job."

"Oh, I see," I said.

"Come again?" Dean responded, not in my direction, his back still turned toward the front lawn.

"Well," I went on, "I couldn't help but notice that you—"

Sam nudged me, and I barely saved myself from saying the wrong thing much too early on in our visit. I shifted to, "I found it interesting that you wouldn't, ah, be intrigued by these vaulted ceilings. At my place, the living room is quite small. And I often wish for a bit more—"

"Wiggle room!" cried Nora.

"Yes, indeed! Wiggle room. This girl is just so smart," I said, leaning down to her and adjusting her glasses. Dean came up to each of us, first Abi, then me. "Dean Wilkinson. Hello, there," he said to each of us as if he was reading a prompt and on his way to report the news: stiff, blue-eyed, long high-bridged nose, narrow hips, small eyes like a porcupine's squinting in retreat. He had broad shoulders and blonde hair (but there wasn't much left of it); otherwise, you couldn't pick him out in a crowd—he had nothing about him, I thought, complementary to Martha. But Nora ran straight into his arms, letting out a grand shrill as he threw her up into the air above him.

The phone rang, and Dean quickly put the little one down and answered it on the first ring. He put up his left hand, signaling to us that he needed space.

That's when Martha said, "Come, we'll go out to the yard for a few minutes. I've got some chicken wings being delivered from this family-owned cookery, all from birds they raise themselves. Those will be here around 4:30. But if you're hungry right now, I can grab something."

"I like that idea. Is there anything we can help with in the kitchen?"

"Let me see— off the top of my head, I can tell you what I've got. I've got tofu prepared for us non-meat eaters, we can throw that into a curry. Dean won't eat it if it has vegetables, so I cook everything separately. He refuses to eat anything that isn't meat. I also made some spinach and feta crepes, vanilla crepes with a salted caramel sauce; oh, my dear, but we'll have to get a salad together. Yes. That was what I wanted to tell you, Sam. What kind of a salad has Eleanor been interested in lately? Oh, and my nephews brought over some coleslaw they made for you and Eli, a family recipe that I'd never even known about."

"This is going to make Nora very happy, Mama. Thank you."

"Don't even—this is what I do live for, and John would have liked us to have plenty of options at the table. And then I think we were going to run out and pick up some of those purple Japanese yams. I like to make this ice cream I think Eleanor will like. I hope! Actually, I don't know if they're yams or potatoes." She had so many things to say, once the right person was around. I watched Sam and her connect while keeping my eye on Dean, who was pacing out front, shouting into the phone. I wondered what it would be like if he was out of the picture. You know, when you meet someone and you don't get a good feeling? This guy was the epitome of that whole genre of terrible songs. If he *was* a song, in fact, he'd be some sort of an anthem. He didn't deserve to *be* a song. I remembered the lines to one song. Dennis Leary (and I was never a fan) sings about a suburbanite slob with all anyone could ask for, a man uninterested in providing anything for anybody outside of himself. But, he'll figure it out one day.

This is such a short visit, I told myself, I shouldn't get myself wrapped up in it. "So it's been a while since you've seen the little one?" I said to Martha.

"Much too long. Much too long. I wish you lived closer, Sam. It would be so nice for Eleanor to be here with us."

"Nora's definitely got her father on her mind constantly."

"Is that so? She's still talking to him. . .in front of you?" Martha whispered.

Sam moved closer to her. "It's okay, I really am not worried about it now. She's processing. I let her talk to him."

"Does she. . .say how he's doing?"

"Oh, I mean she, uh, she says—Martha, I've never really asked her. And actually Joseph was the one who helped walk me through just accepting this as normal."

"Hm. Maybe he'll come and visit us while we're all together. And who knows—he might have some messages. Just don't tell Dean. He'll throw a goddamn fit."

"Martha!" the wretched real estate putz called out to his servant.

"Yes, honey, what do you need? Coming! He's such a baby. Sam. I apologize up front for whatever takes place here. I really do."

"Don't. You really don't have to say that. I understand, Mama." Samentha kissed her mother-in-law on the cheek. "You also don't have to be at his every beck and call. It would help him to lay off once in a while. I certainly don't want Nora to be around any arguing, though."

"It's better that I just take care of what he needs. We'll talk more later. You and Joseph get settled in—and where's this other woman? Abigail?"

"That's me!" Abigail said. It's funny, though: Lately, when I look at her, I just don't recognize her. It's as if she's in the way. As if I've sabotaged myself once again, realizing that I just don't care to have her around, especially after the trip is over.

There was a loud sound over by the front of the house, and Abi and I ran toward it, leaving Sam and the little one out on the back porch. When we got out front, we saw Martha on the ground, next to our car. I ran to her. She was crying there. In a fit, Dean had thrown something at our car, a large branch it appeared to be, and he hit Martha with it. She had a few scratches on her right arm but was alright. Our car, on the other hand, didn't look so great. The bastard had busted the back passenger side window. I looked in through the shattered glass, then down at Martha. I leaned back down and helped her up. I had a heavy feeling in my stomach. I could feel a migraine coming on. What had we all signed up for?

Martha dusted herself off and shook head for a second. She fixed her hair: She kept a small mirror in her pocket and looked herself in the eyes. Sometimes she does this to ask herself for the strength she needs to deal with fuck-face over there, wherever he went. Apparently he was upset that I had been brought along. And he didn't care for Abi, either, even though he hadn't spent more than thirty seconds with us.

We went back into the house to ice Martha's arm, and the little one was supposed to know what had happened. If John's ghost was in fact with us, he was laughing at me. I stood there looking out into the great expanse of pine trees and closed my eyes for a second. Then I asked Martha if she'd give me a tour around their home.

"HERE'S JOHN RECEIVING HIS WINGS at a ceremony on the air base. See him there? So cute. That face. Those shoulders! *Annnd* here's John and Samentha coming out of the church. You can see a few people throwing rice, see? Here's another with Sam and John and the baby. . .in his arms there. Oh, his arms. He was always in great shape. My goodness, do I miss him, I really miss that boy." Martha continued to reminisce sweetly, and that was something I needed to see. Sam had leaned in to me and confessed how relieved she was that Steve hadn't come on the trip. What with all of these photographs of John all over the house. I admitted the same. Concerning Dean, things had cooled down, and when he came back from his walk or wherever he went, he and Sam had a talk out by our car. He apologized, but not to Abi or me. Some people just can't give what's not within them. But I didn't feel safe there, and I was nervous about spending the night. Abi told me I was being paranoid; I disagreed, and this made her even more frustrated that she'd come on the trip. Dean was standing next to Martha by then, kissing her sweetly. That poor woman. Wilkinson. Smilkinson. That smug teardown with his cinnamon-colored beard. I bet he made her do everything on her own, just to spite the fact that she'd take orders from anyone to feel less alienated from her surroundings. I'd never despised anyone more in such a short amount of time. Dean—sallow-eyed, crooked-toothed, grinning fortnight of yesteryear: I'm not a violent man, but I'd love to stuff a hairy beast cock into his mouth and watch him choke on it. Sorry, John, I told myself . . .you had to grow up with that.

But it wasn't fair of me to get so heated up about the whole thing. The secret to any great spiritual battle is to win without fighting. And I know Dean had a difficult upbringing. Perhaps something will wake him up eventually, that prick. I bet his dick's the size of a raisin, but not a plump one, mind you. . .the runt of the litter. You could barely see it with a microscope. A fickle man. Selfish. No patience, self-consumed, no humility. Insolent, poorly paced. In disguise.

"Ah, tell me, Joseph. . .you're the infamous neighbor we've heard all about."

"Oh, I—"

"Your girlfriend's got quite the skinny on how you've stepped in on this situation with Eleanor and Sam. I'm slightly impressed."

"Infamous is too big a word. Neighbor would suffice. I just did what anyone with half a heart would have done."

"Well, now you're being humble, I suspect. Samentha has not once stopped mentioning you on the phone. So we sure do appreciate all the help you've been giving her to make the transition more smooth."

"I couldn't be happier having them next door to me. She's a lovely woman, and Nora is just--she's always surprising me with a knowledge that you can't find in other kids that young."

"We appreciate that. Really, we do."

"I am umm. . .thank you, Dean. Not a problem at all."

"Sam tells us that you're a flyer, or that you were one for the Israeli Air Force. I mean, once a flyer always a flyer."

"Yes, I did fly."

"When was that?"

"In the late 1960s, I flew a French bomber. During the October War in '73, I flew the American-made Phantom. Quite a few times, even the Skyhawk."

"So you're talking about the navy surplus we gave your country in the Sixties, correct?"

"Exactly right. The French imposed an embargo on the State of Israel after the Six-Day War, and the military relied heavily on your country."

"The three billion dollars we give annually."

"Is it that much now? I haven't been keeping track as of late."

"I'm almost sure of it," Dean said, with a lousy smile forming wrinkles around his beady eyes. "Tell me, Joseph—how does it make you feel that we finance the slaughter of innocent women and children on the strip? Raining napalm on all those poor souls?"

"How does it make the Israelis feel when rockets come crashing down from the sky each night, sending thousands to the shelters?"

"Well, wait just a minute, Joseph. There is a huge disparity between your fire power and theirs. Can't you admit to that at least?"

"I hear your point. Let me ask you this, though—what would *you* do if your town here in Bend came under attack by a state located just a few miles from here?"

"You took their country away from them, scattering half a million refugees in Lebanon, in Jordan, Syria, and trapping close to a million more on the Gaza Strip. How do you think these people are doing, right this very second? Shouldn't they fight to get their country back from the Zionists?"

"Who is this 'them' exactly that you're referring to, Dean?" I was about to lose my shit in a moment—but not yet. Not here.

"Take a guess, big shot. The Palestinians—who else would I be referring to?" He was beginning to spit with each word that came out of his mouth.

"The Palestinians never had much of a country to be taken away *from*."

"What are you getting at exactly?"

"I can elaborate if you'd like."

"Please do. Let's sit out on the patio. You can educate me."

"I'm not one to lecture," I said, about ready to quickly devise a plan for how we could get the hell out of there. Dean and I walked out through the kitchen and into the backyard. There was an old swing set that you could tell hadn't been used in a few years.

He began, "The Romans occupied the land two thousand years ago. There were Jews living there who fought fiercely against them. Other countries continued to invade the region for thousands of years, exiling Jews. Some returned to the land. Now, fast forward...the Ottoman Empire occupied the land for a few hundred years until the British received a mandate to rule the country themselves. That very mandate ended in 1948."

"Yes."

"The West Bank was under Jordanian rule for many, many years."

"And when was it that the Palestinians had a country, Dean?" I said. He looked around, puzzled for a moment, thinking about his next move.

I quickly continued, before he had enough time to deliver his next line, "Let me remind you that, in 1948, the UN divided the land, handing both the Jewish settlers and the Arabs their land, on which they could create respective states. To live side by side, in peace."

"And why do you think this happened, Joseph, by chance?"

"I don't follow you."

"That entire movement was a response to the Holocaust, to relieve the burden of guilt the West was carrying."

"Carrying it with them in their blood, in their every breath. Inescapable. Like a heat rash that never goes away. A thorn in one's side. Passed on through generations."

"You're also a poet."

"No need for flattery, please, I shot back. I felt collected still, so I continued. "Don't forget, there was a British declaration before the war, the Balfour Declaration, suggesting the founding of the Jewish state. And the idea was initially formulated by Theodore Herzel as a solution to the pogroms against the globally scattered Jews, to provide them with a sanctuary, or more accurately to allow them simply to return to their ancient land, the home of their ancestors. It was a matter of returning rather than creating. Although, once the UN passed Resolution 242, the very next day. . .the *very next day*, Arab armies invaded the land from three different directions in an attempt to drive every Jew into the sea."

I rose from my chair and walked around for a minute, pacing as I do occasionally. Looked up at the scattered cumulus clouds, wondering when I was going to have a chance to get out of there and drive back home with Sam and Nora. There was a train close by, and it howled.

I carried on once more as I returned to my chair, "We formed the Israeli Defense Forces to protect the newly declared state. The surrounding Arab countries couldn't accept that. They despised the resolution. They'd rather have blood on their hands. Which is still their intention, mind you. So who was it that created the refugee problem, I ask you?"

"Come now, Jo. You've said a mouthful there. And I have to say, if you don't mind, that I'm not convinced. You didn't even begin to answer my own question on how you personally felt about murdering innocent children—"

"If you only knew, Dean. If you only knew."

"If I only knew what? That you have no idea what the fuck you're talking about? A know-it-all."

I was getting flashbacks of my recent arguments with Steve. I saw the pattern. Abi would never see me for who I was. Neither would Steve. And this guy here, I was disappointed knowing that the little one had part of his stink in her. Perhaps it skipped a generation. I could only hope. Sam deserved better than these in-laws.

"Well," he said, "are you going to say something, or what? Space cadet. That's what you are. Your mind is elsewhere. I don't like that. A grown man should be on par, every moment. And your lady friend, she's a catch. But I don't know exactly what she sees in you. I'll be honest. I don't care for you meddling in our lives. But I am still grateful for the compassion you've shown to Sam and Eleanor."

My skin was itching. "Thank you," I said, and we sat in silence for a moment. I could hear the women laughing inside the house. Why wasn't I with them? I'd set myself up, accepted the invitation to sit with this imposter. "Alright, I heard you. Look, I want you to hear me out. If you only knew how many times I aborted missions over the Gaza Strip because a child was spotted playing six or seven hundred feet from our target."

"And what was that target, Joseph?"

"A house. In the middle of a neighborhood. . .with hundreds of rockets stored beneath in bunkers. Don't you see that they place their citizens in harm's way, that they leave us no choice but to inflict collateral damage on them?"

Just as I was about to let him have the worst of me, the women strolled into the yard with us with a look of fright on their faces. They heard us for sure.

"You two were just going at it, weren't you?" said Martha. "Considering you just met, I'm not very happy about that. I'll say it again, I don't like the sound of your voices."

"FOOD'S ALMOST READY, BOYS." SAMENTHA SMILED, leaning over Abi's shoulder. The little one was holding onto my hand, staring up at me. She suddenly jumped into my lap and started to play with my hair. For a moment I began to cry inside; it's just what happens when she's near me.

"Abi, if you and Sam would like to freshen up with me in the vanity wing, we could have some fun now! The men can set the table and get the drinks prepared, and we'll have a little pow-wow in the powder room. Come, you too, Eleanor. I want to get your hair combed, and we'll change those shorts into some pants. It will be just a little chilly tonight. You can count on that."

THE SUN HAD GONE DOWN on the city by the woods. The house was far away from the city; you could hear the crickets chirping loudly. It was pitch-dark outside, with the smell of cow sheds and other livestock carried on the breeze.

I went back to the car to get my wallet, cell phone, and some alkaline water. I had a feeling that, if I brought in the whole supply we'd purchased, Dean would give me shit. *Alright now, focus. Cell phone, flashlight, a few extra pens, my notebook. . .I think I put my shaving creme in with Sam's toiletries. Yes, that's right.* Glass was everywhere in the car, but I'd clean it up in a few minutes. *Just let me grab a few more things.* The extra pair of sunglasses could stay in the glove compartment, and I guessed I'd stash Abi's smokes in there as well.

As I made my way back Abi was waiting by the front stoop. "Did you grab my smokes and lipstick?"

"Oh, I didn't! But I can go back and—"

"No, it's not necessary. But, honey, I wanted to ask you something real quick. Before we head inside."

"What's that?"

"All that arguing, you and Dean. Was it about Samentha?"

"Oh, no, not really."

"I'm worried, though."

"Don't be."

"You alright?"

"It was an emotionally charged conversation for me. I'll say that much."

"Oh, I know you've got way more to say than that, dear."

"He's, uh, well, it's come to my attention that he's not exactly a friend of the State of Israel. He sees moral equivalency between the terror inflicted on the Jewish state and the way the Israelis respond to it. He doesn't even see the difference between terror and legitimate warfare."

"You can't change the world, Jack. Don't try."

"He was pestering me, and I truly wanted to give him a bit of Jewish History 101. But I doubt that his mind is capable of absorbing any of it."

"Hm. Fascinating. Jack, I'm starved. Let's go fill our bellies."

"I'm concerned."

"What? What now?"

"I'm concerned about what he's going to say during dinner. I know he's going to let me have it, and in front of everyone just to spite me."

"Hey, now—hold on, Tiger. You don't need to obsess with this one, alright? Don't ya see? Some people just don't get it. Try not and feed his ego."

"He's a bit like Steve."

"Oh, dear, Steve! Have you phoned him yet? I wonder how the

apartment's holding up."

"He called me the other day, left a message on my machine. I listened to it."

"Has he asked about Sam?"

"Yes and no."

"What's that mean?"

"Well, he told me to tell Sam he misses her face, although he didn't say anything about how the little one. Apparently, Kathy's in town."

"Oh, brother."

"I told him they're not allowed to fornicate in my apartment, not anywhere near it. I don't want a goddamn speck of dust out of place."

"Kathy's a free spirit now. She doesn't need him," Abi concluded, fixing her hair in the rear-view mirror.

"I don't know, Steve is quite a manipulator. One takes what one can get when there doesn't seem to be a more viable option available."

"I mean, Jack. . .I thought Steve was fun when we were younger. I was drunk half the time."

"So was I."

"Jo! Hey, Jo!" Nora called out. No one had ever called me "Jo", and I rather liked it. Way more than "Jack," and more so than "Joseph." And then she came bouncing towards me, and with her the memory of how morning light would sneak into my peripheral vision as I woke from a dream. I'd scoop her up into my arms, and the smell of her skin would make us dance like ladybugs on a trampoline.

Abi decided to head inside, feeling the chill of the June nightscape at her fingertips.

"Jo! I saw some eggs, there were so many. I counted them, but I forgot to write it down. Look over there, if you can see." Nora pointed toward the chicken coop. There was a dim lightbulb hanging from the wooden structure.

"I see, Eli. Do you want to collect them, bring some into the house for breakfast?"

"I think that sounds good, oh yes I do. But maybe I can ask Grampa first?"

"That's a smart idea. Let's go ask your grandfather first." We all gathered around the dinner table. I was worried that Samentha was going to get uncomfortable once Dean started his nonsense with me. He's such a liberal, and in the worst of ways. It's tragic how a word that once held much significance in the future of democracy has now led us to be so closed off from true interconnectivity. A word can have no true meaning once its warped figurative role becomes flaccid. Abi leaned over and whispered, "So what's this guy, a retired general or something?

"I believe he was some sort of civil engineer, but I can't be certain."

There were six of us sitting at the old oak table. The food was hot and ready on the table, and the roast beef and baked potato filled the air in the dining room pleasantly. We were all famished; each day of traveling had especially gotten to me. Abi was on her best behavior for some reason, and Sam was lit up as usual. It always seemed that, even when she was exhausted, still something stirred inside her that gave me hope. In what, I can't be sure—but there was something within her, as there was in the little one, that served my spirit well. Samentha was seated next to Eleanor, I was next to Abi, and Dean was at the head of the table. His wife, sat to his right, and she seemed out of sorts. You could see it in her body language. But she started the conversation. "Oh, I heard that you, Joseph, were the one who really got Sam to stick to this venture to come see us?"

"I can't take credit for much," I said. "All I did was tell Sam that I'd help if need be, and to believe in herself, go for what she really wants. That can be tough, figuring the next step. Especially with a daughter in the picture."

"Joseph," said Sam, "I wouldn't have made it this far without you. You know that by now, don't you?"

"I'm happy to be here, for you." I smiled and felt as if everything was so right. My eyes were glazed over in a sweetness I'd never known. I didn't care if Abi caught me staring for much too long. What's done is done.

"And Joseph, I wanted to, ask you something else."

"Yes, Martha?"

"Sam had told us you were born in Israel. And, like our boy, you also flew for the Air Force over there."

"That's correct."

"She said how you almost lost your life in the October War of '73, when your plane was hit by a missile?"

"That's right."

"Would you like to tell us more?"

"I could, sure." It was time; there was no avoiding it. I just hoped that Dean wouldn't attack me. But beggars can't be choosers at a time like that. "Do you mind if I pour myself a little vino first?"

"Of course, here, let me take care of that for you." Dean poured a few ounces of champagne into my glass. I took a few small sips. Abi nudged me and told me to get on with it already.

"My father," I began, "grew up in a small village in Eastern Poland in the early twentieth century. About a third of the villagers were Orthodox Jews, and they lived strictly according to the biblical laws they'd been taught as children. During his teens, he joined the Zionist Youth movement. It went against everything his parents wanted for him. They were dissatisfied because the movement was focused on a modern creation of a Jewish state, contrary to their beliefs."

"And what would those be, Jack?" Abi nudged me and laughed at how serious I was getting.

"They were simple-minded, motivated by tradition, fear, and faith. . . they believed that the State of Israel should only be created after the arrival of the Messiah. Until then, immigration to the Holy Land was therefore forbidden."

"WHAT'S PHORRR-BID-EHN MEAN, JO?" NORA ASKED.

"It's another word for 'not allowed.' For example, if you asked me for a bite of my roast beef, and I thought you had already eaten enough of your own, I would then say to you, 'Eleanor, you are forbidden to have any more roast beef!'"

"Okay. I see."

"Now, where was I? Oh, the Zionist movement."

"Yes, please. Go on Joseph, we're enjoying this. Aren't we, Martha?" said Dean, which I was surprised to hear coming from him, but I didn't think much about it.

"My father met with these other teenagers monthly, in a hidden place on the outskirts of the village. It was there that he met my mother, Byrna Lipkovitch, the daughter of a local cantor. Unlike my father, Byrna was a petite, blue-eyed blonde with shoulder-length curls and very fair skin. My father had black hair, thin and straight, a square face, and he was very tan, over six feet tall, and athletic. He was quite stoic as well, while my mother was a more romantic type. The two would get together after the meetings. They dreamed about breaking away, starting a new life together far away from the village.

The Zionist Youth movement had an agenda to develop ties with the Holy Land through correspondences via special emissaries who were sent to Poland to encourage immigration to what many years later would become the modern state of Israel.

"In the early twentieth century, the population in the Holy Land was predominately Arab and under the Turkish rule. The British took over the mandate, one which was given to them by the UN, to govern the land after the Turks were driven out at the conclusion of the First World War.

"A decade or so after these events. Zionist Jews from Eastern Europe and Russia began immigrating over, quickly becoming the pioneers who lit the fire of fulfillment, igniting the dream of returning to the Biblical Land, which had been promised to the Jewish Nation some 2,000 years before its destruction at the hands of the Romans.

"These pioneers started to settle the land by purchasing parcels from the local Arab population, and cultivated their land well. The agricultural settlements were modeled after the Russian communal concept, in which all members have an equal share in the land, and the produce that came out of working the land was shared among the inhabitants. Living conditions were rough at best. Many sacrifices had to be made by the newcomers, since they had to leave a higher standard of living behind, even in the smaller villages of Eastern Europe and Russia. This was a landmark settlement.

"My parents, Joseph and Byrna, settled in one of the Jewish communes, named Brenner's Hill, on the outskirts of modern-day Tel Aviv. The area itself became a great producer of furniture and some agricultural prospects. My father worked in the furniture factory and became the chief engineer, designing all the furniture that was produced, and later he designed the buildings that replaced the shacks at the commune. Byrna was the head chef at the commune's dining hall, and she did so with great care. By then, in the early 1930s, there were said to be around 750 members in the settlement. Now, let me tell you that World Zionist Organizations, especially in North America, assisted the fledgling settlement with much needed cash, and sent over equipment for their agricultural endeavors, until the settlement could afford to sustain itself.

"And then a battle erupted between the local Arab and the Jewish settlers, and it turned into a fierce and bloody war. The local Jewish military sent my father to North America, to procure weapons. He had to learn how to speak English in a very short time and surprised his peers by developing diplomatic connections between Palestine and the United States. Through this period, which seemed so hopeless, my father became a key player in the local military organizations developed by the settlers. Defending one's land, property, and sanity from the Arab neighbors was a focus that the members took very seriously.

"I believe it was about two years or so after the founding of the state of Israel, that I was born. I took my first breath on Brenner Hill. My parents named me Izaak Birnberg. I would be their only child. Byrna would spend a couple of hours a day with me, feeding me, and I do remember her kissing me goodnight. But she soon left. I, and countless other children, lived in a separate building and was practically raised by professional housekeepers. The adults were housed in one small room, in a shack nearby. The children attended a school on the settlement and rarely left the settlement itself, since it was unsafe to do so. In later years, they attended universities outside the commune.

"At the top of my class in science and mathematics, I was also a chess champion—the other teenagers couldn't keep up with me. When I finished high school, it was a given that, instead of enrolling at the local university in Tel Aviv, I should be drafted instead into the military for three years. My very last year of high school, I won numerous scholarly awards in both physics and mathematics. Through these competitions in Israel, I was sent to Europe to compete in a few international youth competitions in the field of math. I came in third place at the ripe age of seventeen. And one sunny Monday morning—I remember this so vividly now—my father drove me down to the recruiting station, where I was processed and sent to bootcamp for six months of training. The first phase was a series of exams in physics and physical endurance, under the harshest conditions. I didn't think I'd survive. I didn't think I'd make it out the other end alive, for no other reason than the more I succeeded, the more certain people seemed to despise me, as if I was a threat to others for following through with what my passions were, and at full speed! The mental stress and pressure of the arduous course resulted in a fifty-percent dropout rate within the first year or two of the flight course. While I passed the written exam tests with ease, the physical and mental exercises were much more challenging. But quitting was not an option for me.

"That being the case, after a few months I had started flying with my instructors, soaring through the air. But if you know me at all, you can safely say you knew me when. Although I was determined, I didn't fully comprehend all the rules and often followed my intuition. Although I had my guides, there were moments when something else overtook me. I was. . .steadfast, blinded by my passion for flying. I had almost been kicked out of the program. At times, I couldn't avoid a bird flying into the right side of the engine. No damage was done to the aircraft, but mistakes like these were almost always the end of the program for a student. I got lucky. My instructor saw beyond such incidents, and I went on to my second and final year. By then, I was flying solo and became proficient in handling the French-made jet: one seat, one fighter. Three months or so before the conclusion of my program (and after receiving my coveted wings), only eighty flyers remained in the course."

"Jo? Joseph. . ."

"What is it, dear?"

"I really like your story. Are there any butterflies in it?"

"Well, if you eat more of your vegetables, I'll make sure I put a butterfly or two in there. Hm? Whaddaya think, Nora?"

"I guess. Well, okay. I can do that."

"So, as I was saying. . .ah yes, then came the most precious day of my lifetime thus far, as well as a special moment for my parents. I passed the very prestigious Israeli Air Force flight course with flying colors, and I received my wings. My parents, Joseph and Byrna, stood there with tears in their eyes, pondering how I would be the first of my generation of Israeli pilots from The Brenner Hill commune to pass the test. I remained in the air force for five years, at the end of which I decided to visit the United States. I wanted so badly to pursue my engineering studies on the West Coast. One morning I woke up and went up to my parents and told them that I wanted to study abroad. It was two or three months after I was discharged from the service. My parents said to me, 'Izaak, why don't you take a sabbatical, and return later to enroll at the University of

Jerusalem?' I was moved by their suggestion. So I took this opportunity to make the next move.

"'I guess I could use your connections in California, Dad. Do you think that could be a possibility?' And no sooner than those words leapt from my mouth, my dad and I were discussing his investment in a high-end hotel in Beverly Hills. This would help me with my educational endeavors on a level that most teenagers don't get a chance to take on. I agreed to visit Los Angeles, and after a while I decided on my future course. I packed lightly. . . . A year later, during mid-terms, I was on my way back to Isael, to fly faster jets days after the October War broke out in '73. The tension between Israel and its Arab neighbors was plaguing my every move. They called it the 'Yom Kippur War,' and it caught the Israeli army by surprise. I was met at the Ben Gurion Air Field by my commander, who drove me straight to the barracks. He apologized up front for our meeting under such circumstances. He knew about my studies and my plan to continue my education abroad. I confessed that I loved flying more than anything, but that the stench of burning oil on a daily basis gave me shivers. Taking off, landing, taking off, landing.

"'What's the situation with the next landing?'" I asked the major.

"'Izaak, we got caught with our pants down this time. And I mean it—this round is not going to be tolerable. We'll need each and every flyer to turn the tide for us all. We're not there just yet. You'll be flying night missions in the South, over the Canal. We must drive the Egyptians back—otherwise, we're screwed. *Royally* screwed, Izaak. These guys are fighting with more skill than they've ever had. But they're still no match for what we've got under our belts. You'll fly tonight. You'll lead a squadron of bombers and drop napalm on the Egyptian tanks. Got it? West of the Canal.'"

"'Do I get to sleep for at least a few hours before I climb into the cockpit?'"

"'Yes. You've got a few hours to rest. Now go,'" said the lieutenant as he pushed my shoulder toward the back door and turned to get back to his notes.

"The first few sorties went well, and due to the shortage of flyers I barely slept during the first week above the battlefields. Reserves were called in, but the intensity of the fighting was overwhelming. We had to regain what we'd initially lost in the first few days of the war. Ten days later, the tide had yet to turn. In the north, the situation was grave, with the Syrian Army advancing deep into Israeli territory almost to the Sea of Galilee, north of Tiberias. The military depended heavily on the air force to destroy the advancing tanks. We flew around the clock with very little sleep and not much food either.

"To my own surprise, I managed to visit back home, the Hill of Brenner, for two nights. And that was it, since returning to Israel. Byrna, my mom, and Joseph, my father, were glued to the television set day and night, observing the explosions and, sadly, the downing of some Israeli aircraft.

"Toward the end of the campaign, I felt a shuddering in my plane. The left wing had caught fire. And I knew—in that moment, mind you—that the plane would never land or fly again. Without reluctance, I pushed the eject button, and my body flew into the sky. I watched the jet burn above me, and the closer I got to the ground, the less I felt the heat from the its flames. All I had to do was land and survive, which I did, but not without injury.

"At 2:00 a.m., I lay sprawled in a dune inside Israeli territory. They helicoptered me to the nearest hospital, where I phoned my parents. Being the middle of the night, I'm sure they knew what to expect. In just a few short hours they showed up at the hospital. My right leg was in a cast from hitting the ground, but I had very few cuts, just minor wounds.

"'Do you think I could fly by tomorrow?'" I asked the doctor.

"'Well, flying is a possibility, but you'll need some down time first, son. No need to rush. It'll take time for your injury to heal. Could be months. Your leg is fractured in a couple of places. You'll have a hard time getting into the cockpit of your jet, even after you're feeling better and movement becomes regulated. For now, I suggest that you focus on another career. Besides, we'd like this to be the last war in our neighborhood. Enough is enough. But thank you for your service, Izaak.'"

"BY MID-FEBRUARY, I WAS EAGER for everything to get back to normal. As you can imagine, I was *ferklempt*. But don't let that fool you: I had everything in me to take on the remainder of the new year. Whatever was to follow could be my saving grace. I was enthusiastic beyond belief. My parents thought I was some sort of nut job. But as I was saying, it was the middle of February, and the October War was over by then. I landed in Los Angeles to complete my studies, intending to settle down for quite a while. I changed my name then from Izaak Birnberg to Joseph Brenner."

"Well, then," Dean declared into the silence that followed.

The little one looked up at me and began to laugh, as she had spotted some shreds of beef on my chin and asked me if I was saving that for the ants she'd seen on the front porch. I said, "Yes, of course I am!" and everyone began talking at once.

Martha spoke out first, after my long-winded conversation about myself and my ancestors, to thank me for it.

"That was beautiful, Joseph," said Samentha as she put her hand on my shoulder and squeezed it slightly. Abi was looking at me as if I was out of place, turning her head to the side, squinting as though I was being propositioned to apologize for my elongated tale. But I did no such thing.

"We were just as relieved when John returned in one piece," Martha said, laying her utensils on her plate after finishing up the last bite of her potatoes. She looked in Dean's direction for a moment, then around at everyone and continued, "As I was saying, we were just besides ourselves when our Jon Jon returned home safely. He was flying missions in Afghanistan. But as you may already have heard, he perished in an air accident a few years later." She paused and tears began to fall from her soft blue eyes. Dean did nothing to console her; she sat there in her moment alone, and that was not easy to watch. ". . .Our hearts never did recover, Joseph. And I can relate to the worries that your parents went through. I can. It's something no parent wants to go through. That's what they don't tell you about in school, the feeling of loss the moment they leave the nest. You don't know when it could be the last time you see their smile."

"I'm so sorry, Martha. I feel for you, believe me. My parents called me each night to make sure I was still alive and well. It wasn't easy for them. They told me countless times that it was my choice to become a fighter pilot, but that their peace of mind had deteriorated with time. But they were proud of my achievements nonetheless."

"What exactly were those achievements, Joseph?" Dean asked, not even looking at me, staring down at his plate, picking out the tomatoes from his salad like a child. And before I could answer him he shot forward like a menace and went on, "Your achievements were raining bombs on innocent civilians in the Gaza Strip and Southern Lebanon! They didn't *have* an air force, dammit, Joseph! They had no way to protect themselves!"

I said as evenly as I could, "We were left with no choice, Dean. All we knew was we had to hit targets that the terror regimes were placing among their civilian population. It was them or us." I began to feel a rush, and my hands felt warmer than usual. I was sick to my stomach. Samentha and Abi stared at me with a look of bewilderment, unsure of how to navigate the battlefield about to erupt. You could cut the air with a pair of rusty scissors.

"Joseph, tell me, son, when did you first arrive here? I wanted to ask you, because I somehow forget what that date was."

The temperature instantly fell. "I came in at the end of 1970 for school, returned in '73 to fight in the October War, then left Israel once again to finish my studies. That would have been in 1974. Shortly after that, I began working for an LA record producer who'd started a company in Hollywood."

"A record company?" said Dean. "That makes no sense. What could you possibly know about music? You said you were a mathematician and a fighter pilot."

"Joseph is also a very talented pianist, guys," said Samentha. He's incredible."

"I can honestly say I didn't expect that," Dean replied.

"Well, if you must know, shortly after I got the job, they offered me a CEO, and I virtually ran the entire operation after that and became a major stockholder."

"Did you ever get married, Joseph?" Martha asked next, and I'm sure I know the question that would follow.

"Yes! I married someone right out of college. But she wasn't exactly the one for me. We separated eventually."

"No children?"

"No children, unfortunately."

"I will say, from the way Samentha describes you, we can tell that you adore Nora, and she in return adores you! And in such a short time. Nora doesn't get attached very easily, Joseph. You must know that."

"I'm very fond of her, and I've grown attached to her as well. I tend to be overly protective of Sami, too. Please, don't ask why. I don't know the answer. I think I could safely say that Samentha is the kid I never had, I suppose that's the best way I can describe the feeling of longing tc make sure she's alright. And that Eli is safe as well."

"Regardless of our differences, I'm. . .well, Joseph, Martha and I, we're happy for the extra help," Dean added.

Samentha was sitting at the edge of her chair, smiling the way she did that just made my heart skip a beat every time. And she said, "He even nursed me back to health when I was having those excruciating migraines. Mom, I was just a mess, and he was there. Not to mention that he puts

Steve in line when he gets out of hand!"

"Who is this Steve? The man you're interested in?"

"Well, I don't know what's going on with that whole situation." Sam sat back in her chair and said nothing else. I couldn't blame her, he's a nuisance. Sometimes I wished that he and Abi would run away together, so that I could get back to the life I'd truly wanted to build, with Nora at the top of my list, and Samentha my guiding light.

"And you, Abi?" Martha asked. "You have any children of your own?"

"Oh, no. I don't I don't think I've ever been the mother type. And now it's much too late for me to try. But I've gotten to spend some time with Eli, and she had opened me up to the idea. When Steve and Sam went on their dates, I got to know her while Joseph was babysitting."

Abi ended it there. Of course, there was the whole story of Tom and how their marriage had ended in divorce. But we never get into Tom, do we? You'll have to forgive me, but there are so many elements to this story that I may have left out a few crucial details.

"That's just wonderful, Abi. Isn't that wonderful, Dean? They took care of our Eleanor."

Dean said nothing much, mumbled to himself and forced a smile. I could see in Martha's face that she was getting more disturbed by the fact that her husband had been so cold during our visit so far. She certainly was embarrassed—it was obvious.

"So who is this guy Steve?" asked Dean.

"I met him through Joseph. They're close friends. I told you about him before. Did you forget already, Pops?"

"Oh no, no, I remember. I wanted to know more about him. I'd would be happy to. I mean, what sort of a man is he, that he doesn't come along to meet your in-laws? Should I be concerned?"

Martha said, "I'm glad you're back in a relationship, Sam. We'll meet him one day. Eleanor needs a father figure. It's not beneficial for her growth to be cooped up inside an apartment, raised by a single mother, with no real family at all in that Los Angeles place. . . . Do you mind, Joseph, if I ask you something?"

"I'm all yours. Ask away."

"So I was wondering if you, well. . .tell me if you find this too forward." She smiled as she leaned over her dirty dishes and half-finished glass of champagne.

Dean snapped, "Oh, good Lord, woman, you better not be asking him what I think you are."

"Will you just shut up for one second and let me talk?" she said softly but with an edge to her voice.

"I see! She's got a pair of balls on her after all. I knew I married you for some strange reason!" Dean poked her in the side and ruffled her hair.

Martha looked at me and was about ready to lose it, but she composed herself.

"Do you have plans to go back to Israel one day? How long do you think you'll be in Los Angeles, and are your parents still living?

"My parents still live in Tel Aviv, and they're well taken care of. I fly there twice a year to look after them, make sure their health and activities around their neighborhood are still a benefit in their later years. My aunt looks after them when I'm in California."

Samentha asked, "Are you leaving anytime soon to see them? And how long will you be staying there, if I may pry?"

"I'm leaving at the end of July, and I may take Abi along. I usually stay about a month."

"Joseph," Dean snapped as Martha continued to grow more anxious, especially after telling him to shut up, "I have one more question for you. Do you feel loyal to the State of Israel, or to our country?"

"Well, you see Dean, unlike many other immigrants, I didn't run away from my country."

"What's your point?"

"I mean that many immigrants run from their countries, having been tortured and harassed by their own people, by their own government. When they look back, they feel only bitterness and a sense of betrayal. I left on my own free will. I didn't run away. So I do feel a sense of loyalty to the country that I was born to defend. At the same time, I'm an American citizen, and I love this country."

"But you didn't answer my—"

"Dean," Martha said, "will you stop this already! You're giving me palpitations. Must you always get the answers you're looking for? Joseph is our guest, and you're interrogating him! Enough is enough."

She stood up and began to clear the table. Abi and Samentha did the same. Dean retreated in defeat out the front door, slamming it behind him. I took the little one out to the backyard, and we did our best to count the stars and even sang a song together. She fell asleep in my arms shortly after, and if it hadn't been for the mosquitos and my allergies, I might have cried. But this time, instead, I smiled and looked back up to the sky in both disbelief and enchantment.

CHAPTER TEN

THE WHITE ENVELOPE

"WHAT DO YOU THINK, HONEY—IS THERE ANYTHING we need to pick up from the store before head out to the lodge tomorrow?" Annabelle asked.

Wait! Abigail. Who's Annabelle? That could be a nice name for a dog. I wondered, if I adopted one, might the young one be interested? We could take pictures together on the day we picked up the mutt. What kind of a pup would that girl with the pink glasses like? A small fuzzy lap-dog, or a beastly one the size of a small horse?

"Jaack!"

"*Oh!* I started making a list for the market. Where did I put that thing?" I scrambled around in my suitcase, and Abi continued to make comments and sigh loudly. She wanted me to rush through everything, as if my very existence was all about getting things done in a timely manner for her. I move slow; so be it. I can be a steam engine if I really want something great. But what I want, I'm not allowed to have. . .clearly.

"We don't need your lists. Come on."

"Well, alright, then. Hey, I liked the stairs up to our room—they looked sort of designer made. No? I mean, my father would have been able to recognize that, anyway."

"Your father made furniture, not stairwells."

"He still had a knowledge of all kinds of things—door-frames, cabinets, *et cetera*."

"Look, Jack. I just wanted to say how very sorry I am about how that prick was coming down on you. Since we first arrived, he was all up on you. I mean, what's his problem? A classic redneck, and I just can't stand him. Must we return here after Crater Lake?"

"I'm afraid we do have to pick up Sam and Nora, and then we'll head back down south. But I'm not at all oblivious to how you reacted that lunatic's antics. He's only related to her through marriage. It's not Samentha's fault." Abi was changing into her robe; I myself was off the whole robe kick and instead got sort of obsessed with an old pair of swim trunks and an oversized tank top Sam bought online that fit me perfectly: I love when my axilla area can truly breathe. "La-la-lah-lah—"

"You're really creeping me out."

"What? My shirt or my singing?"

"The *shirt*. I don't like it. I have to say, it's a little odd, Jack. And it's not a shirt, it's a tank top. For women."

"Gee, thanks, I appreciate the flattery," I said, laughing to myself.

"Where'd you get that thing anyway?"

"Oh, well, I just grabbed it last minute when we were packing. I was in such a rush, I think it might be one of yours."

"I don't wear that color," she said, stopped in her tracks, turned around, and looked at me. "It's. . .*hers*, isn't it? You're never in a rush. What are you *talking* about?"

"Really, Abi, I don't have time for your paranoia. We'll be on our way back down South soon enough. This will all be behind us, just one more night. We'll never have to deal with the Wilkinsons again, not after tomorrow, if I can help it."

"Yeah, but who will we all be when we get back home?"

". . .What do you mean by that?"

"You know what I mean."

"Let's get some sleep now. We'll talk about everything at the lake. Turn off that light, will you? Thanks, dear," I said, settling in to my side of the bed.

Abi and I would rarely hold one another while in bed. In fact, we hadn't slept in the same bed together much for over a decade. It'd been a while since we'd had sex either. But that's a whole other story I didn't feel like getting into that night. Perhaps we were the only ones still awake in the house, since I suddenly thought I had gone deaf. The damn migraine was trying to climb aboard the ship.

Even so, I was somewhat at peace. There wasn't a sound, aside from a few crickets outside our window. There was some livestock close enough to the property too, what sounded like cows and horses. Those rural sounds put us all to sleep, along with the humming of the central air unit that started up right as I began to doze off.

After a brief and mostly silent breakfast, Abi and I left. We drove south for about two hours, to the crest of Crater Lake National Park. I parked in front of the lodge and dealt with registration while Abigail brought our bags up to the room. We passed through the A-frame, a small two-story cabin. The lake was a fifteen-minute drive from the lodge, so we wouldn't fuss with our things and instead headed straight for the sights.

At the park entrance, I paid the gatekeeper fifteen bucks, a travesty. After we passed through the steel gates, the road became quite steep. The parking lot was gigantic (if only they had lots like this at Trader Joe's!). What's that all about? I always wonder. Great prices, but the real price you pay is a fender bender while trying to get into your car when you leave.

"Hey, Earth to Jack. Did you want to check out one of these gift shops?"

"Why not? Then we can grab something to eat, you think?"

First, we went into the gift shop, and they gave us a map for free which really made my day. I opened it up and started to read about all the facts, landmarks, other national parks in vicinity to the area.

"Look, Abi. Did you know that Crater Lake is six miles long, and therefore one could circle it in about forty minutes?"

"Just fascinating, Jack. But you can't convince me to try that."

"Oh, balls, you're always killing my buzz."

"That's what I'm here for. What do you say about getting something for the little one? Does she like dolls? Or any sort of winged creatures? Didn't she say something about—"

"A butterfly, yes! Why didn't I think of that? Help me find something with butterflies. Anything, it doesn't matter. We'll each see what we can find, and meet back here at the front counter in fifteen minutes. See ya then," I concluded, and made my way off to find something precious for Nora. After rummaging through everything I finally made my way back to Abi, who seemed impatient already. She had found a set of pencils, a baseball cap, and some napkins. I'd found Band-Aids, a hairbrush, an umbrella, a hand-puppet, and some chocolates. Then, on my way back toward the front counter, I picked up some marbles and a small lamp. I noticed a coloring book down by the sticker aisle, but I'd run out of fingers. I was up to my throat in lepidoptera.

"Alright, we've got plenty of butterfly options here. Now, which ones do we go with? I rather like the pencils, but the napkins could come in handy. She likes hats, though. This is a tough one. Yes. Alright then, let me get out my calculator."

"Oh, must we go through this now? I want to get to the lake, Jack. Don't do this. I'm begging you. Can you hear me in there?"

"Abi, this is how I do things, so you may want to relax for a few minutes."

"I'm gonna buy the pencils for her. I'll meet you out by the vantage point near the restaurant. We can watch the lake far below us. . .doesn't that sound lovely, Jack? Jack? *Jack!*"

"Hold on there. Jesus, I'm almost. . .I got this figured out here." I had started to calculate the cost of all the items, but I still had to figure taxes, and what I could do was subtract the items that I didn't care for, and eventually I'd whittle the pile down to two or three toys. . .what I might just do is, well. . .oh, confound it. I'd just buy everything. So, like a fool, I scooped up the items, dropping a few along my way to the register. I was trying my best to look-see out the windows at how far Abigail had gotten to the vantage point. I thought I could still see her. I was making the kid nervous who was ringing me up, I could tell. I asked if they had any gift- wrapping services, and they gave me two whole rolls of wrapping paper for free, if I promised them that I wouldn't come back for at least twenty-four hours to give them a break. I was glad Abi wasn't around to hear that.

I PUT THE BAG OF BUTTERFLY STUFF in the trunk and made my way to Abigail. My leg was already acting up; just a few hours sitting in the car, and I'm a goner. But I realized then that I had come a long way on the journey. And not just the trip to Oregon: I thought about the first time I saw Nora and Samentha. I couldn't stop replaying our talk out on the balcony, and how badly I wanted to sit down at my piano right this moment and just let it all go through a song for the two of them, something they could dance along to, and maybe even one day the three of us would sing something together.

The air smelled of cabbage and shrimp, and the early afternoon sun was glistening right above the lake itself. Slowly it descended along the waterline as I made my way closer to the vantage point. I wasn't the slightest bit hungry, but I knew that, once I got inside the restaurant, that would all change. Just get me around the sweet smells of vegetable lasagna or a steaming pastrami sandwich, and this Jack is a happy boy.

Abi was seated on a small rock at the bottom of the stairs of the restaurant. We looked out to our next destination and held hands for a few minutes. That was unexpected. Suffice it to say, just as I got to thinking I could enjoy this a little longer, Abi sighed about how my hands were clammy, and that I had the aroma of glass cleaner. I was offended; the God-honest truth was that I'd bought a very plain cologne at the gift shop, and I rather liked it. It was called Moonshine Musk, and it reminded me of my youth. I didn't think I'd offend anyone. I put a very little on my beard, even took off my shoes and sprayed my socks and a little down my pants just in case I got gassy. I didn't want Sam or the little one to smell my desperation upon our return to Bend. I was thinking too far ahead.

Eventually we made our way back to the car and drove down to the cascade after circling the lake for a while and hiking a trail or two. The cascade wasn't part of our plan, but we could see it from a distance. When we got there, we found a few folks, with their dogs, walking back and forth between the pine trees, branches reaching up to the sky.

I reached for Abi's hand but as soon as I got a grip, she broke away and began to run ahead of me. "Race ya, Jack!" she shouted as she sped off without me.

I called for her, unable to move very fast myself—my leg wouldn't allow for it. And she knew that! But I enjoyed my trek toward the falls, alone and out in nature with my thoughts. Chipmunks and hawkmoths scattered about the trail before me. I didn't know who I was anymore, but at the same moment I felt that finally I'd found myself at the crux of a great deluge, fully aware and accepting that it was what I wanted.

I had made it to my destination, whatever that entailed. Here I am, I realized. Lately, I replay that one night in my head over and over again, just a few hours after I first met Sam and the little one. I look out my bedroom window and asked myself, Joseph, what the heck are you doing, feeling these silly feelings? You're a man, not a wimp.

But then I ask, Am I a coward, though? And I look around at the lights of the city and down at the streets, at people passing one another saying not a word. And I listen for just a minute, scratching my beard with my fingers, chewing on a rubber band in the other hand. I wash my face a few times so I can relax a bit. Play my piano for a bit, but not long enough to come up with anything worth remembering. I walk back to the bathroom mirror and look at my incisors, straighten my eyebrows, glance at my wrinkles. I look into my own eyes as if there's another answer in them, the secret in my reflection. I think about how, just a few years ago, I began making other changes in my life to prepare for just this moment. You might say I'm a bit sappy for a man of the great October War, but if you must shame me, then I am obliged to accept the sentence. If you must know, what I said to myself was, *Look. I'm changing my life. I've changed my life. I've brought Samentha to me. She'll never believe my story. But one day, I'll tell her. But only if she invites me onto that level.*

Oh, Jesus, I found Abigail. Time to get back to business. She stood there looking out into the water. I hoped that, before I got close enough for her to see me coming, she'd slip into the water, and I just happened to be distracted by, uh, by this—oh, yes, this Butorides virescens, page 65 of my handy bird guide, printed in 2006 and edited by Jonathan Alderfer!

What a last name, tragic. It was the best buy in a while, for me, something I could really dive into before we got back to Los Angeles. Shouldn't the Butorides virescens be more along the Willamette River?

By the time I made it over to Abi, I'd read through a few more pages and had plenty I wanted to share with her, though I knew she wouldn't be the slightest bit interested in my research. The Certhia americana was also one of the many on my route here. Its birdsong is almost inaudible, says the book.

"Hey, Abi, did you see all those chipmunks on your way over? They were quite something, weren't they?" I shouted, but she didn't respond with more than a smile, as she turned back to watch the rushing water below us. The falls sprayed us with the cool mist of yesteryear, reminding us that we were standing in front of Niagara Falls on the American side. . .getting soaked from the distance. But it didn't matter how wet we got, soaked this was the cascade, and the air was warm. Nothing else mattered. We found a comfortable place to sit and didn't move an inch for almost an hour. We breathed deeply the confessions of the forest air as small creatures appeared, affectionate, slipping by us like Lady Macbeth—possessed by our keen imagination of what it would be like to be standing, instead, within the falls, as if nothing harmful would transpire and we would become the falls. Like the sensation of being in the shallows, but grander.

"YOU KNOW, JOSEPH, I COULD REALLY USE some of those snacks right about now," said Samentha, leaning back in her seat, smiling at me with ease as her hair blew in the wind. I always forget how beautiful her eyes look when the sun hits them—a color I can't exactly describe. There we were, back where we belonged. Such a rush. Sam played around with the radio, trying to find something fitting for our newfound freedom from all the schmucks we'd left behind. Although John's parents would always be in the picture, for Sam at least, if she decided to stick around, perhaps I'd see them again.

"You guys want some snacks? Let me see, shall the little one pass you my backpack? Nora. . .Nora you awake back there?" She hopped up from behind my seat and started to giggle, teasing us both with a pink scarf she was waving around.

"Jo! Where's your backpack?" cried the little one.

I had completely spaced out. "It's down there, right by your feet! But first, my dear heart, I want you to put on your seatbelt—we're driving, honey. You have to be safe."

"Thanks, Joseph," said Sam, rubbing my shoulder for a second.

"No problem." Just then a classic song came on the radio, and it set me into an even better mood—if you can imagine that even being possible!

"Oh, I love this song, Joseph! I used to listen to these guys when I was in college. I can't believe this is playing on the radio! No one ever plays the good stuff."

"And everyone knows who The Stingrays are by now, don't they? Well, maybe only musicologists like me, but I think the seed has spread over time."

"Seed? What seed?"

"Well, with the internet we all have access to this smorgasbord of tunes. It's an endless archive, that I can assure you."

"The name of the song is 'Melting With You'!"

"Mom," said Nora, "I need a snack now. I've been listening and listening and listening, oh boy. You guys talk too much." Sometimes she really cracks me up.

"So, what's in the bag? Oo, this looks good!" said Sam, rummaging through the miniature supermarket in my bag. She pulled out a few exceptional items, I'm sure, but I see what. You might find this odd, but I so loved overhearing the racket she made as paper and plastic bags smothered one another. Eleanor started squealing; she was hungry as well. I hope that what I'd packed was sufficient for their appetites; I hate to be unprepared. You never know when you'll need an extra pack of gum, a bar of chocolate—even a pair of scissors comes in handy. Especially on the road, mind you.

"What'd you choose there, Sami?" I asked, keeping my eyes on the road.

"Nora, why don't you tell Jo what I picked out. This will be good for your vocabulary. After all, school is always in session here with Mr. Brenner."

And I couldn't be more pleased! Tell me, will I frighten her when I tell her about all these feelings? The sweet and curious sprite stayed in her seatbelt like a good little girl, and read off the items to me that Samentha held in her arms.

"I see. . .a sandwich! And a mango, two mangos—oh, that means one for me! I see cookies! Mm! Mama, I need a cookie now. I waited, didn't I?" Nora started humming a tune and kicking the back of my seat. I loved every goddamn second of it. I even sang along and, simultaneously and to my surprise, Samentha began singing along. To say the least, I've been used to lonesome town all these years. And oh, let me tell you, these sweeping views of holy groves so green, as if I'd never even been to this land before my eyes. And like the sun, I float to them, my two poems here beside my body. Breathing the same air. And all I can think about is playing them a song, constant as if I were on a flight to somewhere I'd never been.

Yet all of this felt so familiar to me. The last bit of fog was approaching. It was as if we were drifting again into the trees—the feeling from before, when we first drove north together. I remember hearing bells in the moments of silence, which weren't many if you don't mind me adding that. Here I am, the conductor of this steam engine, with the guidance of these two silly gals. I kept thinking, if I stopped now and turned back around, that we could be home. We could be home. We could be home. . . .

The last trek through these forests will always remain, in my heart, a time I wish would never end. I'll never forget any of it. Even the parts that were rough around the edges. I wondered, all these years, if by chance the signs were all around me and somehow I missed them. And all this time I thought I was paying attention. It's almost a bit out of an old film, one that you saw as a kid but you were much too young to make sense of the true meaning behind the director's vision. And I know these elements intimately, mainly for one reason: Working in the record industry for so long, you tend to make sense of how the role of the artist is the nectar of humanity. A song can mean something to the musician because he or she is lying down with the devil to compose an otherworldly representation of a feeling, a longing for someone so deep that only through song can that sort of soul-wrenching hysteria change shape, merge into a thing of beauty instead of anguish. But what was the analogy I was making to the whole universe of movies and such? Well, you get the point, I imagine.

"SANDRA, I NEED YOU. UH, IT'S JUST ABOUT MIDNIGHT. Or maybe it's the middle of the day, around 2:00 p.m.—I can't be sure. I'm a mess. I was just sitting at my desk reading some poetry, and I got a knock at the door. But you're not going to believe what arrived, you're not going to--will you come over? I hate to be needy. Just come to my place. We got back from the trip earlier than planned, earlier today. Earlier. . .I was a different person. And now I can't even make sense of what's going through my head. But I did something big. And all I can say is, be careful what you wish for. Just come over. Okay, bye now, Sandra." The message ended in a beep. She had reached the end of her friend's voicemail, that beep somewhat louder than she remembered. A flustered yet strangely kinda blissed-out woman was embarking on a whole new territory.

But it's not my place to tell you what's about to happen. I know the story myself, though; that's the only way I've been able to sit here and deliver such a wild-eyed fairy tale.

Samentha was crawling back to the sofa when Sandra buzzed her from downstairs. Samentha unlocked the front door and barely made it back to the sofa before Sandra got to the apartment. "Sam," she exclaimed, "you worried me half to death. What in the heck are you up tonight, my darlin'?" she asked, staring at the pale-faced girl with smeared makeup and bloodshot eyes, her hair disheveled.

Sandra had no idea how to deal with it. "You want some coffee?"

"No. I mean, yes. I'll take some. That'll be fine. Is that what I want? Sure." Samentha began to shiver.

"Oh, this has got to be a whopper. Tell me what's going on before I die!"

"If anyone's going to die tonight, it'll be *me*." Sam reached down to take off her socks and threw them onto the dining room table.

"I'm listening. What is it? You must tell me. What is it that could be so terrible? Do I get a hint at least? . . . No? I could start asking you questions, and you could nod or shake your head. . . . Oh, great—well, don't make me do all the work."

"Oh, Sandra. Read it!"

"Read what? Are you getting evicted or something?" Sandra asked and spotted the letter on the edge of the sofa. She leaned over to pick it up.

Who'd have known such a morning would come: a reawakening. I felt sick to my stomach, and oh, how the rain is getting heavier. Out the window, I could imagine what the two of them were going through as the storm broke their reality into pieces—how a few lines, a dozen or so words, can shape our entire world, the one each of us lives within, from our bedrooms to the bathtub and out into the living room. A stairwell becomes a dizzying contraption to our cars and off down the block. I like to drive around from time to time, with a playlist on repeat.

The rain was pouring down heavily by then, and Samentha was sitting there looking out at the black sky. She saw a shooting star amid the thundering, abysmal sky. But was the sky in fact, more bewitching than ever? Had our thirty-something heroine missed the point completely? Or was it I, Joseph. . .Jack. . . Izaak. . .who had missed the point? It was all so obvious; I don't know why I hadn't ever spoken up.

Sandra started to read the letter. Good lord, Sami was right. It was no ordinary transmission. She tried to keep her hands from shaking as she looked up at her friend. "Sam, I'm going to read this out loud, and then you'll punch me in the face so I know this is real. You got that?"

Samentha nodded silently.

"Alright, then." She read it out loud, but Samentha didn't punch her, didn't move at all.

Sandra sighed. "You're a stranger in a strange land," she whispered.

"And it seems you've been. . .been matched to an older man whose name you may have spoken once or twice before."

"A million times before," Sam whispered.

"A zillion times before. And this very moment, you have been given something. . .something remarkable. Undeniable, even."

"God help me."

"It's a perfect DNA match," said Sandra with a touch of laughter, and she got up to grab something from the dresser in the hallway. She knew where Samentha kept her cigarettes. They each lit one and took a few short puffs.

"Do you think this Yakov Brenner is Joseph?" Sandra asked. "I thought his name was Izaak. And what about Jack? Who is this guy? Didn't you tell me he went into some long argument with your father-in-law when he disclosed all the inner workings of his childhood, his real name, all that stuff?" Her eyes slightly closed, she was trying her best to analyze Sam's facial expression, but her friend had nothing to say.

"Alright, let's slow down here. You want we should do that?" Sandra asked.

Samentha shook her head. "Ask me again," she said.

"Ask you what again?"

"Ask me if I think it's him."

"Oh. Okay. Do you think that Yakov Brenner is your neighbor?"

"No! I don't think so. I know it. I've been waiting far too long for this. What do I do? Joseph is my biological father. That makes him *just* a father, not a sperm donor, though, right? What do I call him in the morning? Which name do I use?" A sort of thundering escapade was gravitating closer and closer to my heart. And Samentha got dizzy—it must be that whole migraine thing.

Samentha continued, as her friend remained in silence, covering her mouth with both hands, "Look, Sandi. How do I tell him what he already knew was there? That he already most likely is feeling this in his heart, but he wouldn't let his head admit it? Where does this leave *us* now? I'm his *daughter,* in legal terms. Is a sperm donor considered a father? Is that what he is? I'm carrying him inside me. . .with every fiber of my body. He runs in my blood, Sandra. . .he and I are connected biologically. And I couldn't be happier. . . . Oh god, I think I'm going to barf."

"No, you're alright. Sorry, I'm freaking out, too. I need to do a better job at keeping you on your toes. Come on, let's sit over here. You're panicking! Don't panic. *Breathe.* There you go. Breathe again. There you go, see you're alright."

"I'm his daughter. Me. The last person to ever win anything worthwhile. Is this. . .can you, um, tell me if I'm crazy? Just get it over with. Tell me I'm shit. Tell me this isn't happening. Tell me! Tell me *now!*" Sam fell to the floor and said nothing else, but she was breathing deeply.

"There you go. You're gonna do this," Sandra told her, kneeling down, holding her hands.

Sam muffled her voice in a pillow.

"What's that? Don't do that. Let's go now, sit up straight. Look at me. I'm here. And you're now going to get excited. Alright? Get excited. This is what you do when you find out the best news of your life. This is what happens when you're happy. When you're complete." Sandra pulled her up gently and wiped the tears from her face, adjusted her glasses, and smiled deeply into her friend's eyes.

"I'm him."

"I know, dear."

"He's me."

"You got this."

"What's the meaning of the word 'father'?"

"I know. It's okay, just let it be what it is. This was already happening. All the wheels were already in motion. He was coming for you, and you knew. So that's why you came here. That's why we met. That's why you hate your job, and you hate your life, and it's all coming together. Because you went for what was already happening inside both of you. Yes, that's right. You can smile now. See? It's just what you asked for."

"We even share the same migraines. So, what's the meaning of the word? F-Father. Father? God knows I don't need one. I raised myself practically alone, with the help of my mother and grandparents. I was an accident, and *nothing*. An *accident*. Just an accident and nothing more. How do you think that makes me feel, to know all of this? Very confused—but at the same time I feel like I have been given a chance to be reborn, in his own eyes. In his own heart. Between him and me, me and him. We're the same person. Are you listening to this nonsense that's coming out of me?"

"It's the most beautiful story I've ever heard. Truly. You're making me jealous," Sandi told her, wiping away her own tears.

". . .How do you think it will make *him* feel? When he, you know, when he realizes. . .that he created me, and I grew up from just a wee one. Just like Nora. Without a father. He never knew what he had done. I grew up from a little girl to the woman I am now, all because of some. . .some accident. Like, I didn't have a choice in the matter, and neither did he. One night with my mother, one passionate night to cure the rest of them, forty years ago."

"That's quite a while. Your whole life. Wow. I just—I don't know what to say."

"Sandra, he is *such* a sweet and sensitive man. I've always felt attached to him, and I never knew why, until tonight. I lost forty years of a loving connection. Of happy birthdays. No happy birthdays. Christmas alone, crying by the fireplace with my mother. No memories of *us*. No riding a tricycle, none of him dashing behind me, being picked up from school . . . showing off my dad to my friends. Being comforted during the hardest of my days and nights. I was missing the one who gave me my own life. And I don't. . .I don't resent him. Not at all. What would be the point? He didn't know. I do feel resentment towards my mother, though, who never even tried to discover who my dad was. She didn't even give *me* the chance to know. All she cared about was herself. She didn't give me a choice."

"Here, baby, drink some coffee." Where did one begin, thought Sandra, in such a situation. And she thought of Eleanor, about to discover that she had a grandfather but didn't know it yet. Although she knows just as well. . .she's known all along. She was following John's messages from the afterlife. The girl with the pink glasses already had an idea of what was going to happen; she just didn't speak her truth in the same language as we do. "Sam, Sami. . . . what's in a name?"

"So much," said Samentha. "Like the fiercest of calypsos. Our minds are a *place* now that we can inhabit. Together. Sam and Joseph. A place where earthquakes are manufactured. A place where honey and snowflakes are born. As if Mephistopheles grew wings of jelly and stitched them into my heart!"

She got up and walked to the living-room window, looked out past the front of the building, and realized that I, at that very moment, was watching her every move. And she would have known this all along the way, if she had only stopped doubting herself. But I did the same thing. I put her on a pedestal in my soul and didn't know how to tell her that what lies within this humble exterior of a man is actually a woman, one with a child and the kindest of hearts. The same heart as mine.

"Samentha, who are you talking to?"

"Oh! I was just talking to. . .um, I'm not sure actually. I just came to the window because I heard a song. It's, well, a song in my dreams. Sometimes I wake up singing these. . .these melodies. Half alive."

"Come again?"

"Don't pay any attention to that. I was listening to a song out on the water, trying to sing along. No need to rhyme, to spare them a little time."

"See, baby, your love for those two creatures is just divine, ain't it?" Sandra said.

"In my wildest dreams. . . ."

"In your wildest dreams you wouldn't ever have imagined this would be the case—that a gentle man like him would enter into your life, harmonizing with your daughter and with *you*. Its brilliance has unfurled, dear Sami."

"I'm trembling. Do you think that he'll refuse this connection? He'll be scared, won't he? That's too much pressure."

Sandra chuckled. "Something tells me you don't have to worry about that."

Samentha nodded thoughtfully at that. "Joseph is from Israel," she went on, "and he's a Jew. Does that make me one now? A Jew. I'm a Jew. Who am I? This means I have family in Israel, and the surrounding areas. . .of all places, Israel. Until I met Joseph, I couldn't locate Israel on the map--I mean if you asked me. It's just another speck on the globe. I know nothing about that country, and even less about the people who inhabit such a place. From a legal point of view this is pretty straightforward, right? Factual. I mean, it's what it is. But my life will never be the same from this moment on.

Do I put his name down on my documents, paperwork, whatever it is? His name will be next to mine, *as my father. From now on.* I have so many questions I need to ask him. And I wonder if we can answer them all in the next forty or fifty years."

"Sami, do you know for sure that Joseph and Yakov are one and the same person?"

"Well, no," said Samentha. "But I'm 99.9 percent sure, and I'm pretty certain that that last decimal point will be here by morning. But I'm not really here as Joseph *listening* to all of this, mind you. I just know these things, because they're written in my blood."

"Want me to spend the night with you?" asked Sandra. I can take Eleanor to school, and then I'll talk to Victoria over at work and tell her you're much too 'sick' to come in."

"Yes! Yeah. Can you? I would appreciate that so very much. I need you here tonight, Sandra. I can't be left alone with Nora."

With nothing more to add, Sandra got up and put the dishes in the sink. Samentha grabbed some extra blankets from the hall closet, and a pillow from the bedroom closet, and spread everything out nicely on the sofa.

"I do have a fancy for sleeping on couches," she whispered. "Don't ask me why."

They embraced for a long while, in utter silence. They had run out of things to say. Now it was about to get real, more than just an illusion or a prayer.

And although they made their way through the remainder of the night, as the hours dragged on Samentha became a bit more frantic, frozen, so shocked by such candor that she couldn't make much sense of things. Sandra had fallen asleep in a moment, and Sam went down to the street to pace around beneath the lamplight. And she began talking to herself out there by the gutter—the stinking gutter, urine and old clothing tossed about on a lane going west. She couldn't see the moon; where could it be? She started to call out to it, hoping that it would appear to her.

"I am bewildered. . .dear God!" she whispered. "Help me make it through this night, please! Curtain down, music faded away, tomorrow a new horizon, new beginning, and at the age of almost forty, I'll be born again. . . ." And then she fell silent, stood there leaning against the lamp post, watching the few cars still out pass by a few blocks down. No one would drive past her; it was much too late. Everyone was already asleep in the neighborhood, no one to see her standing alone and completely out of sorts. But she felt very much alive.

The white envelope is ubiquitous. Courage and fortitude had consumed her, but what was to come next would have to be confronted soon enough. She felt as if, in some way or another, she had predicted all of these miracles. It was almost as if she were on a stage—some drama that her grandmother would have enjoyed falling asleep to. Yet while on the stage, she felt emotional, vulnerable, and almost confused. Because she knew, deep down, that once she got off the stage and was in Joseph's embrace, there would be no need for such fears. It was all in her head. Even so, she felt the urge to let go of a few old wounds that needed to bleed through so that they might finally disappear for good.

There was a sense of tranquility, and even if the night had consumed her—the trip, John's death, her and Nora's arrival to Los Angeles—the truth was she'd asked for all of these things, and once more her heart consumed her, *ad interim*. What ended with this night stayed behind her, vast like the abandonment she'd felt as a child. And what with autumn soon to arrive, gone was the wretched memory of darker times, a system of errors to be forgotten. The inability to comprehend these sensations encompassed dimensions she'd not yet identified.

And finally, with much disbelief and episodes of full body tremors, sleep came. Samentha was perfect in all the ways that a woman can be. Within all her insecurities lay a tender being. She was an angel at my doorstep.

She could still hear the murmur of traffic passing by the apartment, someone's stereo blasting from a car. And then she awoke from her thirty-second nap, looked around the room, and began to hyperventilate. But as soon as she got up off the couch, she was able to catch her breath. For a moment she thought she was being dramatic and wanted to forget the whole thing. Stash the envelope in the closet? Or in the tool shed down by the landlord's rose garden? Think little about it for a few days, perhaps a few weeks? Months? Could she last a minute without thinking about the envelope? No. But she felt that she had to get back into her old routine and not say a word to me about any of it.

Well, as you may have predicted, Sam did indeed hide the envelope—overnight, that is. In the morning, she wanted to make Sandra a pot of tea, some blackberry crepes, and bacon. But as they started to get all the ingredients together, Sam said screw it and phoned in a pizza. It was that kind of a morning. I very much wish that I could have been there.

"So where is it? . . . Come on, I know you hid it somewhere. Go get it. You want *me* to go get it?"

Samentha whined, nodding very slowly. But she wouldn't tell Sandra exactly where. There's nothing to worry about, though. Sandra knew exactly where to find it: undisturbed, face-up, on Samentha's stack of books next to her pillow. She grabbed it and admired how, no matter what was going on in her friend's life, she always managed to make her bed. Well, they did both sleep on the couch, but even so, she noticed these things about Samentha, who took care of things that were most important along the treacherous path we all seem to be tumbling down like upward-swimming fish in a golden lake beneath a crescent moon the color of Nora's eyes.

Sandra opened the envelope again and sat there contemplating, reading it twice. She could see how Sam was gazing out the kitchen window above the sink; it was a captivating view. There were willows, and beyond them miles of Trichocereus macrogonus var. pachanoi. I used to grow them myself when I was in my thirties. Their blooms appear only when the moon comes out to play games with the constellations above. And their bursting clusters of spider-like blossoms are quite fragrant. The scent is so wild that, when bees get caught in the pollen of those steady stamens, you won't find them unwilling to share the soft, fluffy nectar. Instead, these bees tumble and fight as if it was their last meal and all their children were already full.

But there was something happening in Samentha's apartment, an event far more important than the neighborly love of flowers. Although not indifferent to the storm inside her, Samentha, I wish I could tell you how badly I want to watch you grow old.

That's the nature of this woman and her daughter. . .a category unlike any I've yet witnessed. As she dozed off, she began to imagine how she'd tell me about the letter. When I closed my eyes I could see her clearly, almost more in focus than in real life. I think she can see me, too.

"JOSEPH, YOU'VE GIVEN ME SO MANY opportunities to get my life back together. It's been a long year."

Samentha was pacing; I was trying to catch her eyes as she passed me, but she was shy that afternoon, and I had been up all night thinking about our trip. Maybe I'd gotten three hours of sleep. You can really feel it in your face, as if someone threw a volleyball in your direction and you failed to see it coming.

"I got a bottle of Manischewitz wine," I had said on the phone, "if you want to celebrate our trip. Why don't you get yourself washed up, change your clothes, come on over. I'll play us a song!" It was the first thing I did when we got home last night, I was aching for those keys beneath my fingers.

"I do love to watch you play, Joseph," she had said. "Will you play something for me as soon as I come over?"

"I--right this second? Don't you want to. . .get ready first? . . . No? Well, that would be great, then. I can do that. Let me just—"

"What if I came over now, and you we could spend a little time together? I could sure use one of our talks after that unsettling *but* incredible trip. It was a dream, Joseph. Really. I'm sorry about Dean and Martha. . .that whole thing."

"Good riddance. . . . Say, have you heard anything from Steven?"

"Nope. And I don't plan on reaching out to him, either."

"That sounds like a plan I can get behind. We can start a new trend. It will feel like our birthday! Or New Year's Eve."

When she came into the apartment, showered and dressed and looking wonderful, we embraced and she whispered, "I don't know where I'd be without you, Joseph. From the moment Eleanor and I came here, you were at our beck and call. First, I thought you were kind of strange though."

"Did you?"

"I-I really didn't understand your intentions."

"Ah. I see. Was I unclear about them in any way?"

"Not exactly. I was kind of broken. Inside. So anything nice that someone did for me felt like a threat. I think that's what was happening."

"That's one thing you don't have to worry about with me, because I'm broken, too."

"You are?"

I nodded seriously. "So I feel for you. This bag of bones is exhausted, but I've got enough energy in me to build a. . . to, uh—"

"Build a glass castle on the ocean?"

"I like that idea a lot!"

"So do I. Thank you for your gifts."

"No, no. You have provided me with the most beautiful gifts of all. Things I don't even deserve. Like a friend. A companion. . .not that I have any romantic feelings for you—it's not like that at all!"

"Oh, for sure, and I don't have any romantic feelings for you either. I put the pieces together eventually. You never had a daughter, and I never had a father. So, we kind of, well. It was meant to be."

"But the truth is," I admitted, "I get nervous."

"Really?"

"What, you can't tell?"

"I can't be *sure*, no. Well, at moments, I can sense you're lingering in a thought, and I've heard you cry. . .a few times."

"Have you? You have not."

"Yeah. You were on the phone. I was. . .eavesdropping. Sorry about that."

"No need to apologize. A man will cry at times. That's inevitable." We walked out onto the balcony and watched the neighbor's laundry scatter around as a huge gust of wind blew the undergarments and dishrags into the air before us. A sock landed on my knee, and Sami was hit in the face by a very large bra. We laughed and got to talking as we usually do. We couldn't help ourselves. But I knew that she still had something to tell me. She handed me the bra and asked me to put it on. I asked if she wanted me to take my shirt off first.

"Do whatever comes natural!" she declared. So I took off my shirt, and she began laughing so hard that she fell out of her chair. I put on the bra and was reaching down to help her up when little Eleanor ran out to us, jumping between us and screaming at me to take off my bra. When I had, Nora tried it on herself; it was quite a sight.

But the little one was soon getting sleepy again. First she began to doze off in her mother's arms, but she awoke shortly thereafter, crawled onto my lap instead, and was snoring almost immediately.

"So tell me, Samentha," I whispered.

She whispered back, "What's that, Jack?"

"Aha-ha. Yes, Jack. I felt there was. . .something maybe bothering you earlier? When I first met you at the front door?"

"Yeah."

"Yeah?"

She nodded. "Mm-hm. There is."

"Alright, then. Should we put her in bed or on the couch?"

"No, she can stay there. If you're comfortable with that. She sleeps so deeply anyway."

"I'm up! TV time!" said the little one, and she jetted back into the apartment and began rummaging through my DVD collection.

"Hey, there," I said, "now that the little one is entertaining herself in the living room, we can get back to business. Spill the beans. You know I'm a good listener."

Sam looked me straight in the eyes and opened her mouth but said nothing. I stared at her for a moment and then began to chuckle, and couldn't help but smile so wide that, eventually, she began to laugh out loud. And how contagious is her laughter!

Good lord, that's a Lichtenstein! blared the TV. Nora's favorite thing in the world is to lie, belly down, in front my TV, watching Bernie Lomax meet his ultimate demise. I have to admit that silly movie has always set my day in motion. I turned to Sam, and she was standing on her head, legs were drifting about above her, with the bottoms of her toes covered in a sooty hue. I did what I thought she'd like me to—grabbed my piano cover, covered myself in it, and snatched a pair of scissors from the kitchen counter. I plopped down next to her on the patio, cut out two holes for eyes and started to coo like a ghost.

"Last year for a costume," I said, "I was an alligator. Abi never liked to dress up with me. One year I made her a costume, and she put on half the outfit, leaving the shoes and top right there on the floor of her living room. What a bitch. She didn't care for Christmas, either. I'd buy the tree, and she's reluctantly help me bring it into my apartment, huffing and puffing the entire time. And then when I gathered all my things to decorate, she made sure to be out of town on one of her trips. Abi reminded me a lot of my grandmother's old boyfriend—"

"Joseph!" Samentha cried as she pulled off my ghost costume and jumped into my arms.

I held her for a bit, singing quietly. "Will you tell me what's going on in that head of yours? I may be intuitive at times, but I'm not so great at test-taking."

"You're my dad," she said.

". . . You're kidding me." I couldn't bear to look away from her face, as I thought I might burst into some joyous bellow. I didn't want to scare her; maybe I should act indifferent at first? No, no more of that.

"Which means that you're indeed my daughter?" I asked.

"Yes, I'm your daughter." She reached into her pocket and produced the letter. I read it and could barely breathe.

"Well, then! That makes so much *sense*. I thought I was losing my mind there for a while," I confessed, but kept eye contact although I did feel bashful.

"...What do you mean?" she asked.

"I have to say, real quick, I knew all along," I blurted out.

"You *did?* You *knew?* How—wait, who told you?"

"Well I didn't know about this," I said, lifting the letter, "but I knew there was something different among the three of us. I didn't know how to put it to you, exactly. And I wanted to sit with it for a while. Surely I had my doubts. I figured one day you were gonna forget to call me, and not want to bother any more. I thought one day I'd wake up and you wouldn't be there anymore. And I'd never get to see Nora again."

And did I feel the confidence rise within me, as if I was a new man. My joints felt lubricated, and my lungs somehow clearer, as if my organs were expanding in size, the same way the Grinch's heart grew three sizes that day, Christmas morning, when the little ones down below produced melodies as if it was all somehow planned from up above. Not that I believe in God or anything, but she's an okay kid if you ask me.

"Really?"

"Huh?"

"Joseph, you were saying you knew about us, even before the letter came, even before we met?" she said, playing with her hair and biting her nails.

"Yes, I knew that you were coming for me. I'd had dreams about a woman and a young girl moving into that empty apartment, ever since I moved in there actually."

"That's how you knew? How many dreams did you have of us?"

"So many that, eventually, I lost track of what was really happening. I started having flashbacks from when I was a flyer. The list is endless, dear. Don't worry. I'm not worried."

"I'm a little sensitive, Jo. I also figured you'd forget about me eventually, go off with Abigail, and I'd be stuck at this apartment, wondering where I went wrong in life. Probably just stay with Steve since, hey, at least he'd be someone to keep me company, even if I could barely stand him."

"This is funny, eh? Us, here."

"You're scared?" she asked me.

"Not in the slightest."

"Why?"

"Because, my dear, it's not so complicated. I overthink, this is true. But eventually I learned that you had the same bad habit."

"And the same migraines."

"Those, too," I mumbled to the funny kinda porcupine of a heart that beat before me.

"And when you eat something slimy, doesn't it make you gag?"

"Yes! Oh, of course--you see, who wants to eat a giant hot booger?" I asked, imagining that the little one would get a kick out of that analogy.

"That sounds like an absolute nightmare. A huge load of snot."

I am one lucky man, one lucky asshole. Speaking of nightmares, I believer in something these days. You could quote me on that. Sam and I, we wove a mighty labyrinth and escaped the inevitable doom we'd both accepted as our lives. The two of us, we did this. Maybe we were desperate, but rightfully so. It was all written before our time, and who can argue with that?

Nature herself, often so cruel, cold, and blind, may try her best to sabotage Sam and me. But I don't take it personally. Although I had begun to wonder about John's parents. I don't see how Samentha ever fit in with that family. Dean was a close-minded son of a bitch. Strange how two so very different people would come chose one another—although I did the same thing for half of my adult life.

Sam's folks are—Jeez, I don't like to do anyone a dishonor, but they seemed old and confused. After thirty years of marriage, they're just dying inside, waiting, waiting for the day to come to an end so they can sleep off their awful conundrum of a marriage. Why do people even *get* married? I wonder. Emilie and I, well, I should have been there for her. I was too young and more than a bit confused about what I thought I wanted. I know I've made it sound like I got a good amount of tail in those days, but that was never the case. I loved one woman only, and I lost her. Somehow she came back to me in the form of Samentha and Nora.

You could say, sure, some of us get lucky and fall in love accidentally, with a whole new lease on life. I breathed this all into creation myself. Aren't you proud of me? I chose these variations, rather than let such a metamorphosis backfire on me.

"I like the way you walk, Samentha. It reminds me of myself. And I've never been particularly keen on myself—although now I think I just might be getting there."

"Ready for some fun?" she asked.

"Pretty goddamn ready, if you ask me."

"I knew you were going to say that, Dad." And as soon as those words left her mouth, I spun around like Venkman in his red jacket, right there next to that fountain in the middle of New York City, and there's the gentleman who wears a red blazer, across the way from him, spinning in circles. That Elmer Bernstein is still, to me, one of those composers who never wrote a bad score.

"I'll miss you calling me Joseph. And you did call me Jack, earlier, which I thought was funny. Don't you?"

"Yeah. But we can call each other all sorts of names now. And. . .I'm glad that Abigail is out of the picture. You deserved better."

"You deserved better too, than Steve. And even John—I mean, was he even good to you?

"I don't feel like getting into it."

"That's alright, I'm here to listen when you're up to it." Those were sensational amendments. The petal of a rose glides along the veranda. . .perhaps just a balcony to most people, but I watched that rose drift right into my palms. I'll draw the slate out, sincerely reincarnated. I continued, "Samentha, there's something you should know. We're going to find you the man you've been searching for. I assure you, he's out there."

"No one's going to want me. I have too much baggage," she said, looking back at me.

"Ah, but don't we all fall short of character at times? We yearn to make it to the finish line in some sense, because if it weren't for our desires we wouldn't have a thing to look forward to. And looking forward is quite an exceptional line of business. If life were perfect, no one would have anything to complain about. And to kvetch is what you gotta do, take it from me—builds character. We challenge ourselves when we attempt to think differently."

"I know you're mostly into classical music, but did you ever take a listen to that one group from the Nineties. . .some film director's name was in the title."

"Title of the album, or title of the group?" I asked my daughter. *My daughter.* This ain't just a news flash. I may have pulled out my back along the process, though, and I'll need a massage. There's a place called Jolly Foot in North Hollywood that sure does the trick. I should take up the martial arts. Get a hair cut?

"I think it was something about twins."

"Twins? What, you're thinking of having another child?"

"No, silly! Well, actually," she said, deep in thought for a moment.

"Oh, Cocteau Twins?"

"I think that's them, yeah!"

"Look, if I'm going to be your father, I want you to know this. . .I will never let you down. Whatever is mine is for your consumption."

"Consumption?"

"Oh, well, I'm running low on words, Sam. I'm trying here, though." I scratched the back of my neck a few times. I was getting nervous but not exactly sure why.

"I am you," she said. And you are me."

"Yes, my dear. Dare we call it delirium?" I was feeling confident, feeling the rush of fireflies in her belly. To make a confession like that—how absolutely remarkable.

She added, "Papa, this absurd fluency of our kinship has me floored. Its gleam is wise and rushes through my bones." We were suddenly poets, ignited. I smiled down at Nora where she stood between us. She poured the rest of her soda out onto Sam's shoes, and the three of us laughed, a sound so majestic it was as if a scroll had fallen from the clouds with a get-out-of jail-free card for all three of us. After all that Sam and I had been through, it came to the small white envelope I was still holding in my hand. We are resurrected. She needed a father, but not just a father. . .she needed a friend, and someone who could understand her way of life, which so resembled my own inner landscape.

"So what happens next?" she asked.

"How about we trust each other? And promise—each of us—that we do this together. We promise one another that, from now on, we'll never be apart. And we see what happens. Whaddaya think?"

"I like that idea. And, with this trust we are building our new life together. . .right in this moment."

"We built all of it yesterday!"

"It's that simple?"

"Why not? Now let me see those smiles. . .stay there, we'll take a picture. I need to set this up and put the timer on."

"You have a lot of cameras? I used to have so many. I bet some of them still work," she said. The little one was next to me, and I showed her just a minute or two of some camera smarts I had under my belt.

"Hey, dad."

"Yeah, Samentha?" I answered, my chin trembling. If she called me "dad" one more time, I'd try my best not to choke on my response.

"You think I'll meet someone? Like, a good person, who will want to take care of me? Who will let me live my life and share every single moment with him? I can get slightly needy when it's the right person, someone who takes me into their arms."

"If there's one thing you should know, it's that you can't put a price on that smile of yours. It's like a—like a fresh-pressed record, a steaming hot vinyl just oozing with delectable tracks from a time so very long ago, centuries back, *so* long ago that it sends shivers down your spine, and as the needle penetrates the vinyl, and the first song begins to play, we dance. We dance like sons of bitches!"

"My god, Dad. . .you've got a dirty mouth. I guess we have a lot of other things in common we haven't noticed yet. I'm an avid reader myself. I just get self-conscious about my voice."

"Well, your voice is splendid. And as far as my talking dirty, we never did get to have that talk about the birds and the bees, did we? Your daddy was quite a catch in his earlier days. But he was a very misunderstood kid."

"We have stories to tell one another. I feel like I've been asleep my whole life. Tales set against the backdrop of this shit-hole of a city."

I agreed. "Darling," I said, picking up Nora and planting a big wet kiss on Samentha's cheek. She often lets her mustache grown-in, which I rather liked. So I get a bit of a prickle at times against my own beard. In my head I'd always dreaded this moment, because wanted it for so long. But now that I'm arrived here, it's even better than I could have imagined. But I'll tell you something: Lord knows I need a goddamn shower. I'm ripe as hell, and I've got a family to raise.

About the Author

Eli Makover was born and raised in Ramat Gan, a city adjacent to Tel Aviv, Israel. In 1970, following three years of service in the Israeli Air Force, he relocated to New York at the age of twenty.

Shortly thereafter, Mr. Makover moved to Los Angeles to pursue his studies at California State University, Northridge.

While his passion for piano playing began at a young age, it evolved into a lifelong avocation encompassing writing and composition.

Upon completing his studies, Mr. Makover embarked on a twenty-eight-year career with the State of California, from which he subsequently retired.

He is the father of three children and grandfather to eight grandchildren. He currently resides in North Hollywood, California, and enjoys spending time with his family.

This is his first novel.

www.ingramcontent.com/pod-product-compliance
Lightning Source LLC
Chambersburg PA
CBHW030534310726
48979CB00010B/1902/J